Fields

MW00812312

Dedication

Mary Joann Carlton

May 3rd 1937 – January 22nd 2015

My dear mom

So sweet and full of love

The Avant-Garde

A Boom Generation series

Kelly Fields

kelthscreations.blog

Catherine Fields – editor
Diana Cojocaru – cover art
Daniela Vasquez – inside art

Other books by Kelly Fields
Millennium Earth
Guiding the Stars
Crossing Rivers

The Avant-Garde is a work of fiction. Names, characters, places, and incidents are the products of the author's imagination. They or are used fictitiously therefore any resemblance to actual events, locales, or persons, living or dead, is entirely coincidental.

Preface

Two atomic bombs fell on Japan, a year later the High Council from the Pleiades began sending 144,000 Wayshowers to Earth. These Wayshowers were sent to help bring in the new Earth. While experiencing some important events during their lifetime, they learned to live consciously, and to receive instructions in their dreams.

Eighteen years after the second great world war, these Avant-Garde Wayshowers are ready to go to college, or to be drafted for another war. They remember hearing the stories about the last war and they aren't too keen about being involved in any war. While this new war is starting to unfold, the High Council will be on track with the plan of the ages, and it's now in full swing. These Wayshowers were told by the High Council that there will be Avatars along the way to help them.

In what is nearly a twenty-five year period that an adult life is lived, marriage, children, buying houses, therefore full of exciting surprises, and challenges. The Wayshowers performed their mission, which is to learn, and experience this time of their life on planet Earth. They certainly contributed to helping make the planet a better place to live and after working in their occupations, raising their families, they are ready to transition into the next phase of the plan. They will receive some help, but it won't always be easy, and after they are gone the people on Earth will need to carry on without them.

As they move into the final phase of this plan, they will continue to learn, and to be prepared for more of the adventures that are there throughout the galaxy.

Avant-garde

Councilor Ambrosia

CHAPTER 1

A flash of bright light is noticed once again on this blue planet called Earth. "What are we to do?" Was the question asked by these alien types of people, from a faraway place? None know yet, this hasn't happened before on Earth. Sure they stepped in to foil man from learning too much in a point of his advancement that would only lead to disaster. But now, this! Another atomic bomb exploded, but this time on their fellow humans. On the planet the people were given this description of the events.

"Sixteen hours ago an American airplane dropped one bomb on Hiroshima... The force from which the sun draws its powers has been loosed against those who brought the war in the Far East." President Harry S Truman.

Although these two atomic bombs were the first dropped on people they were not the first atomic explosions. That happened on July 16, 1945 at the Trinity Site, in New Mexico. This was a big moment for the people on Earth, without knowledge of the fact that they were being watched from far away, and because it's hard to hide a mushroom cloud that big. Things on Earth are going to change and change drastically.

In the constellation of Taurus, of the Pleiades star cluster, the Pleiadians were watching us. These Pleiadians have an interest in what we were doing on earth. And when the mushroom clouds were noticed the High Councilor Ambrosia called the Chiefs of the Seven Sister Clusters to an emergency session. There were Elders and Chiefs from all of its seven star clusters.

"Order, order let the High Councilor speak." said Leto the announcer.

"Welcome my fellow Pleiadians we all knew this day would come."

Leto the reader said "Now is the time to break the seals from the books so we can review the plans that were made by us eons ago."

When they were opened they then discovered that when the people of Earth obtained the ability to destroy the planet this countdown would begin. The question is can they prevent the humans from destroying the planet or do they even want to?

Chief Hermes asked "Your Grace do we really want to help these humans?"

Ambrosia answered "why yes Hermes, we do, they are our fellow Pleiadians, and we made a pledge that when this experiment came to an end we were going to help prepare them to come back home."

"I know your Grace, but look at how savage they are; they are fearful, judgmental, hateful, and greedy. Do we really want to bring them back here?"

"Yes we do, the plan is to change them back, and also to learn lessons from their Earthly experience."

"Well alright Your Grace let's get on with it then."

Leto then said "stage one has begun and we will need to send Wayshowers to prepare humanity for the last generation. We are to ask for volunteers to inhabit humans on Earth to help guide them. These Wayshowers will enter their Souls and reside in their hearts."

Hermes asked "How will they enter the heart and soul?"

"In order to enter the heart and soul a particle beam will be used. It will match the heartbeat and energy vibration of the human. The only trick is they will not remember going there or where they are from."

Ambrosia then said "right and they have to learn their way and read the signs that are to be sent to them over the next several decades."

Leto sadly ended with "The only thing they will know in their hearts is that they don't fit in, with the world they are a part of."

The call went out for volunteers to go down to Earth and the number was to be 144,000. Tens of thousands volunteered to go at first and it would take almost 20 years to accomplish the total number of 144,000.

Ambrosia said to Chief Dardanus "you have a question?"

"Yes, I do your Grace, wouldn't it be so much easier to use our advanced technology? In that way we could simply show up and demand that they change?"

Leto then paraphrased from the plan, "The reason that can't happen is; because the Soul is not technology, it is the spark that operates the heart of the body it resides in."

All were in agreement and the High Council was ready to move on.

Reading further Leto said "To start preparing the Souls to come to Earth, first parents have to be selected and although this is done scientifically there are no guarantees that they will all be successful. These Souls are pure light that will be sent to Earth on a particle beam, and that is a one way journey."

Dardanus then said "Your Grace, What are the scientific ways to select these humans?"

Leto answered for her and said "We are to evaluate their heart's vibration based on how they love."

Ambrosia said "Thank you Leto".

Leto finished the reading with "when they arrive, they will enter into the mother's womb, and this will happen when the baby kicks for the first time. The Soul will then become a part of the baby's body, it will then act as it's consciousness, and will reside in the heart."

Hermes said, "How do we prepare these Wayshower's when they are on the planet?"

Leto read "We will send Avatars to help guide the development of their children. This will be done through friends, family, educators and in dreams. These people will be adults and some in influential positions on the Earth. These humans will only be the ones who have asked to be filled with the God element in some way."

Ambrosia said "Okay the council will need to send a group of Elders to help carry out this part of the plan."

Hermes asked "Leto how many will we need?"

"At first only 70,000 will be needed to accomplish this, and we have seven years to get them in place."

Ambrosia said "Then let's send out a decree to enlist these volunteers."

In this part of the plan, the Elders will come from the star clusters, and will go and inhabit people from the continent that they represent. They will not enter into people of high office or leadership, but some will be as close as an advisor to those people. This is not the same as the Spirit becoming the baby. In this the Spirit will co-exist in the Soul, but still reside in the Heavens and only guide the humans in dreams and visions.

Seven fleets of ships are ready to depart to Earth one to each continent, full of volunteers of Elders and Wayshowers. When they arrive they will set up a base on the other side of the moon. This will keep them from being spotted and they will start processing who they will visit. The selection is not random and the candidates will be people with a high heart vibration. Much the same as when the Virgin Mary was selected. These people will be open to the will of God or whatever name they use for the Source. The night will be perfect for dreams and then the transfers will happen. This will enable the Elders and Wayshowers to fulfill their missions.

The Miller and Brown families are typical Americans that range from hard working to privileged. They are one of the many families that were chosen to bring help to their home planet Earth. They just weren't aware of it, at least not yet.

Dr. Paul Miller MD is glued to the radio listening to the reports on the war. That's when the announcement came on from the President that Japan was bombed by atomic means some sixteen hours ago. The President felt that this was the right thing to do, to end the war, and prevent a full scale invasion of Japan. Paul's wife Lucille was sitting on the couch listening to him explaining the merits in doing so. She then reflected on when she met Paul at the University of Auburn. He was finishing his internship to complete his medical training and she was a sophomore studying to be a nurse. Now she hopes that this will be the last war on this Earth.

It's a wonder that Paul would become a doctor, since his dad is a Senator, and his dad is very headstrong politically. While spending a good portion of his life in Washington, D.C., this made him want to come home to Alabama so much that he looked forward to their summer vacations, and he told his dad that he wanted to go to college in Montgomery.

He couldn't take his eyes off her, "Mr. Miller" she said "what procedure would we use for…" He turned to answer her question and his heart was alive with feelings he didn't know he had. He knew right then that he had to meet this beautiful woman with those big brown eyes. Therefore the next time he saw her he was going to ask her out, "maybe a picnic" he thought?

Well that chance happened just a few days after they met while walking to class. Paul said to her "Hello there Mrs. Miller" she looked at him very puzzled. He was always making jokes. He just had a carefree spirit about him. Then when he noticed her smile, he knew that she was right for him, and then proceeded to ask her to go on a date, "how about a picnic this Saturday? I've heard the weather will be sunny and not too hot."

"Mr. Miller, are you asking me out on a date?"

"Why yes I am, I would like to get to know you better, and we can discuss school if you would like to."

She didn't know if it would be proper to accept, but she

did want to learn more about this handsome man. "Okay, what time are you picking me up?"

"I'll pick you up at noon and we'll drive to the lake."

Their courtship was interesting, he was very confident, and always knew what his plans were. While she was always thinking about another time and place that she wasn't sure what her plans were on this planet. He was a southern gentleman, in every way, and she would pretend to be a good southern girl. It's not that she wasn't a very good person, she was, she just had questions about a lot of the customs in the world.

After a few dates then the time came to meet their parents. He asked her "how about dinner with my folks this Friday at the Boathouse? They will only be in town for a week and I would like for you to meet them."

"I don't know, what I should wear, is it formal?"

"No, just dress the way you do for school, that's what I'm doing."

Paul's dad was a very loud and proud man. He also would spare no expense to make sure his guests were happy. "So, this is the lovely Lucille I've heard my son talk so much about."

"Glad to meet you Senator." she said.

Then he took her hand and kissed it and said "you are every bit as lovely as my son described."

Paul's mom was used to letting the Senator hog all the attention. She was very content to go at it slowly and get to know Lucille over time, if she were to marry their son. Lucille wondered if his mom liked her since she was so quiet. She then asked Paul "does your mom like me?"

Paul answered "I believe if she didn't she would stop my dad from talking so much. That's how she learns about people by listening to the answers from his questions."   "Okay, I'm just very nervous."

"You're doing fine and who you are makes me so proud."

"We will need to travel to Atlanta and meet my parents. My daddy is working extra hours on a new helicopter project for Bell Aircraft and they can't travel right now."

"That's okay, the drive will do us good and it's only a few hours." Paul said.

"You are very understanding and I really want you to meet my dad, I think he'll like you, especially since you will be a doctor soon. I guess the engineer mind only see's the bottom line in life." Lucille said.

"I sure hope so because I have so many things to talk with him about."

In Marietta, Georgia about 35 miles north of Atlanta you will find the home of William and Jennifer Conley.

"Oh Paul I'm so excited for you to meet them, how much longer before we will be there?" asked Lucille.

"I would guess within the hour."

She said happily "great that will give me some time to work on my make-up."

Paul just smiled and said "dear you can't make that face any more perfect than it already is".

"You say the nicest things let's just hope that doesn't change anytime soon." she said rolling her eyes.

They have arrived. Paul lets Lucille out to give her mom and dad a very big hug.

"I've missed you so much and I have so many new things to share with you." said Lucille to her parents.

Dad shakes Paul's hand and says "my daughter seems to

be very happy with you".

"Yes sir, she is one of a kind and I knew that I would have to meet her." replied Paul.

"That's good to hear, after dinner we can go into my study, and enjoy a glass of Scotch, with a fine Cuban cigar. I bought them on my last business trip down to south Florida" he said to Paul.

"Sounds great sir, I enjoy a fine cigar and drink after dinner, and we do have a lot to talk about." Paul said looking at Lucille.

Then dad answered with "that we do my boy, we sure do."

After asking her father for her hand, it was now time for him to plan on when he would ask her the question. On the drive back home he didn't let on about getting her parents approval. He did however do a lot of planning on when and where he would pop the question.

"So you and my daddy got along great I see," Lucille said to Paul.

"Yes, he's a fine man, and very intelligent with all that engineering talk. I could understand most of it but it sure is technical from a mechanical standpoint." he told her.

"Paul you could talk medical to him and he wouldn't understand most of that either, the main thing is you two got along." Lucille said with a sense of pride in him. He then gave her a very sheepish grin.

Graduation time and Paul is ready to start his life with Lucille. "There's a nice French restaurant in Birmingham that I've heard about. How about we go there Friday night for some dinner and dancing?" Paul said.   "Don't you have to prep for your graduation and aren't your parents coming to town this week end?" she said.

He smiled and said "Yes, all that is true, I just want to see you dressed up, and to take you somewhere special before my big day gets here."

"Okay let's go then, you know how I like to wear something new, and try a new restaurant." she said excitedly.

"So we're set Friday night and we will need to leave around 3:30 then." he confirmed.

Birmingham the big city in Alabama, seeing it Lucille said "wow the traffic sure is different here than in Montgomery."

"Don't worry dear I have reservations and we will get there in plenty of time." Paul assured her. He was very happy to hand the keys over to the valet of his new Chevy Fleetline Aerosedan. It was a graduation gift from his dad, the senator.

After a delicious dinner of French cuisine, and some vintage wine, it was now the time to ask her. She looked at him holding his hand and said "what is it with the smile on your face you have been acting strange since we finished our dinner?"

"Lucille, I have something to ask you." he replied.   "Yes!" she said as if she was giving the answer to his question before he could ask it.

"Well, let me ask the question first." he said grinning. She had a good idea what he was about to say and she prepared herself to answer. He got up and got down on one knee and she started to cry happy tears. He said "I guess you know what this is about then." So he gently grabbed her left hand and pulled a little ring box from his coat.

"Yes, yes, and yes!" she said.

He then said laughingly," well I guess the ring did all the talking."

Their wedding was magical; her family spared no expense

for their darling daughter. It was a garden wedding and the beautiful oak trees at Cobbs Lake in the springtime were more than spectacular. Lucille's father said to her "my little girl is getting married and I have a surprise for you after the wedding."

She said "daddy you are full of surprises, and I can't wait to see what it is." She was so very nervous and trying not to think about all the people there.

Her father took her hand and walked her down the aisle. "Who gives this woman's hand in marriage?" asked the minister.

"I do, said her father."

The minister asked the bride, and groom, these questions "do you Lucille Conley take this man...?"

She replied with "I do".

He then asked Paul "and do you Paul Miller take this woman to love and...?" Paul said "I do."

Then the minister concluded with "you may kiss the bride."

Half way around the world, waiting to see if he will have to lead his men into battle, onto the island of Japan is Sargent Connor Brown. The day was hot on the island and the men were preparing for the invasion. Connor was a natural leader and made the rank of Sargent with only two years in the Army.

His men knew that he would always support them as long as they upheld their honor as soldiers. He was the kind of man that did his job as compassionately as he could. Then the news came that President Harry S. Truman ordered the dropping of two atomic bombs on the citizens of Japan. So now they had to wait and see if Japan would surrender.

"Should we continue to fight, it would not only result in an

ultimate collapse and obliteration of the Japanese nation, but
also, it would lead to the total extinction of human civilization."
Emperor Hirohito

On August 15th, 1945 Japan surrenders. The news came a
week after the bombs were dropped. After the announcement
the soldiers started to return home to their countries and then to
get on with their lives. The Miller and Brown families were ready
to do just that.

"Men it looks like we are going home so let's start
preparing for the move" said Sgt. Connor.

"Yes Sargent. I bet you're ready to go back home to your
new wife," said Corporal Jones.

"Not soon enough, my friend, not soon enough." He would
be home in about three weeks.

His wife Elizabeth was home trying to keep up with the
family farm and Connor new that she was doing the best she
could to help with the family chores. She got along well with his
mother, who was teaching her to cook. Connor and Elizabeth
grew up together where they attended the same church. They
were married only two months before he was drafted. Connor
thought about signing up but knew Elizabeth wasn't too keen on
him going to war. That doesn't sound too strange except the fact
that he honored her wishes, was a very more open minded man
than most, and respectful of her.

Growing up on the farm in eastern Indiana, was a life
designed to achieve honest, and respectful citizens. His dad would
go to him, to make sure the fields were plowed, and planted. Even
though he wasn't the oldest son, his brother Robert was 3 years

older, and was a mamma's boy. That was ok with Connor, who loved the outdoors, and was very good at working on the farm machinery.

Even though Elizabeth's husband Connor was in the Army, she secretly didn't approve of the war, and couldn't understand why so many mistakes were made that seemed to facilitate its continuance. In that time you didn't speak out against anything your country did, even though you did have a 1st Amendment right to do so.

The day is here that Connor arrived home and gets a well-deserved hero's welcome from his family and friends. His young bride was teary eyed, she was so happy he was home, and not injured. "My dear sweet Elizabeth the thought of returning home to you is what kept me alive." he told her.

"Well, worrying about you being over there fighting didn't help me stay alive. If it weren't for all the chores that needed to be done around here, I probably would have spent more time worrying about you. But, now that you're home, let's celebrate by having friends, and family over for a big picnic next week." she said in what seemed like one breath.

Connor smiled and said "now that sounds great, I can't wait to show you off now that I'm back from the war."

It was a cool evening, the chores were done, and they were both very tired, but not sleepy. Then Elizabeth asked him "honey what it was like over there?

I know you would write, but you didn't really go into any detail about what it was like over there."

He answered with "well, mostly it was horrible, and I do want to put it all behind me. The food was scarce, and not very good, but when you are so hungry you don't think about it then. I met a lot of fellow soldiers from many parts of the country and some from different countries too. Some of the men were so young and a lot from poor homes that I felt the need to help them whenever I could."

She looked at him and said "you are so kind and I think that is one of the things that attracted me to you. "Thanks darling, you're already helping me forget the war." he said with a big smile.

"Wow, this sure is a big turnout, seems like most of our family and friends are here." proclaimed Connor. Elizabeth said to him "Well, they are anxious to see you come home, and find out what it was like overseas."

Now Connor was a very kind and polite man so when asked about the war, he would tell them about the day to day stuff but, didn't mention combat. He went on to say "It's so nice to see the new family together other than at church. Darling what do you need me and my brothers to do to help?"

"Probably just keep the fire going and unload the food when people arrive." she instructed him.

The picnic was a welcomed celebration after four years of war. Connor was able to find out if any friends went and what happened to them. *Being home sure is great* thought Connor.

CHAPTER 2

Operation Crossroads was a series of two nuclear weapon tests, conducted by the United States at Bikini Atoll in mid-1946. They were the first nuclear weapon tests since Trinity in July 1945, and the first detonations of nuclear devices since the atomic bombing of Nagasaki on August 9, 1945. The purpose of the tests was to investigate the effect of nuclear weapons on warships. (Source Wikipedia)

Both of these expected mothers were having the same type of dreams, at first neither could understand what they meant, only that they seemed to give them hope. Their children were born Paul Miller Jr. and Margaret Brown, both in 1946. Now with these children born, the plan from the Heavens has begun!

Susan White, who is Lucille's best friend, is a couple of years older, and is looked up to by her. This was a beautiful full moon night in Alabama were Susan was just relaxing on her front porch sipping a glass of her favorite wine. Combined with listening to the crickets and the bull frogs sing it just seemed to put her in a different state of mind, maybe even in a trance. Before she turned in for the evening she took a deep breath as she looked to the sky and noticed how beautiful the moon was and thought how wonderful her life is.

The moon helped put Susan is in a deep sleep, dreaming of magical people, and places. This is the time to implant part of an Elders Spirit into her heart. An airship from Celaeno passes by and stops above her home at around 1200 feet. Then a light particle beam comes down, around 6 inches in diameter, and fills her room with light. While this is happening she is in her dream flying around some majestic mountains covered with snow, her heart is warm, and filled with pure love.

She then meets this visitor from Celaeno in her dream who says "Susan you have been chosen to be an Avatar and to help guide your friend Lucille in teaching little Paul."

"What will I teach her and what's an Avatar?"

"I will reside in your Soul with your Spirit. Then thoughts or ideas will come to you at times that I deem appropriate."

She thought that was weird, but had a good feeling about it, and knew as time went on she would understand it more. Although she will remember this she will not tell anyone what happened.

She wakes up the next morning with a feeling of power in her Spirit that she can't explain, other than the knowledge that she will be given what to say, or do to guide Lucille. She looks at the Sun rising, she wants to communicate with all her heart, then feels a sense of oneness with it, and all of nature.

Now this will be a good time to find her best friend Lucille to share these feelings of power, love, and hope with her today.

Then they meet at Lucille's home, Lucille is still nursing little Paul, who is ten months old, takes all of mom's time, and attention. Susan's two little children are in school, thereby leaving her available during the day to help her friend with her first one.

Washington D. C. is where Lucille's in-laws live, where Pauls' dad is still serving in the Senate. Her parents are living far away in Atlanta. She is grateful to have met Susan and she would visit her at least once a week.

While Susan was sitting at the kitchen table with Lucille having tea, she decided to share her dream with her. Susan said "I dreamed I was flying around these snow covered mountains and it all seemed so real." Susan did leave out the part with the visitor.

Lucille shared with her that she was having some strange dreams of her own too. "I too was flying and could move at great speeds through the universe. I felt as one with the galaxy that I traveled on."

Susan would just listen and nod her head in complete agreement with everything said.

Lucille said "I feel like these dreams were something that happened before I came to this Earth."

Now Susan was seeing how this was going to work.

Elizabeth's life just got a lot busier, sweet little Margaret has learned to walk at 11 months and she goes everywhere. "Sweetie come to mommy I need to clean you up for dinner, your daddy will be here soon."

It was a very busy day on the farm, Connor and Elizabeth, are tired, and ready to relax. She thought about her dreams and then remembered the nightmares that he would have about the islands in the South Pacific.

Elizabeth said "It's so good to have you back and now that we have little Margaret this place feels so much like home."

A full moon and the wind blowing in from the north made for some good sleep, when an airship from Maia arrives at around 2:30 in the morning. This bright light momentarily enters the room, then Connor is startled thinking he's back in the war, but when no noise follows he just goes back to sleep.

"Ready to beam down" said the visitor in the ship.

At this time Elizabeth was dreaming about being a leader in another galaxy, so her heart was full of love, and hope.

As she dreamed the visitor said to her, "I am here to join with your Spirit to help you raise Margaret. She has the Spirit of one of our fellow Pleiadians from the star cluster named Maia."

Elizabeth was not frightened because this visitor seemed familiar and she understood the message given. She continued having her dream of planets, the bright galaxies, and being a leader of them while she travels around.

The next morning she remembered the dream, and the feeling she had last night had happened once before, when Margaret had first kicked in her womb.

During breakfast she tells Connor "I had a strange dream last night."

"You did, and what was it about?"

"Well it's hard to explain, but here goes. I dreamt I was flying through the galaxy and this time I was a leader. I met a visitor from another planet and I was told that Margaret's Spirit was from their planet."

"Interesting we will talk about it tonight after dinner, now I need to get to work."

She then kissed him and said "okay goodbye dear."

A fleet of ships from the Pleiades have dropped off their entities in North America. Then on their way back home something goes wrong. One of the ships crashes over the New Mexico desert and this is a very tenuous situation. The others fly by and pick up the crew and return back on their flight.

A local rancher sees the crash happen and goes to investigate. When he gets there he sees a disc shaped craft buried in the ground. He then drives into town and goes to the Army Air base and meets Maj. Marcel and tells him what he found.

After investigating this, the Army said it was an UFO. Then later retracted the story and said it was a weather balloon. The "weather balloon" was collected and flown to Fort Worth, Texas and eventually ended up at Wright Army Air Field near Dayton, Ohio.

One thing is for sure is that some technology was captured, reverse engineered and used towards advancing military projects.

When the Council were made aware of what had happened they immediately went into an emergency session to determine what would need to be done.

Sinon said "Your Grace we should put the plan on hold until things blow over."

Ambrosia then responded with "our records show that this had happened before and we will be patient."

Darnanus said "but the humans are using atomic bombs and starting world wars, and they are in more danger today than ever before."

Lycus said "The timeline has begun and the grand plan needs to continue."

Ambrosia finished the conversation and said "right we will

use the United Nations to help stop these wars from happening again, after all we were successful in doing this many millennium ago."

So now it's time to watch the humans in the U.S. run with the technology that they captured.

The engineers at Bell Aircraft have been developing the X1 to break the speed of sound and after witnessing the UFO's speed they believed it can be done. Capt. Charles Yeager accomplishes this on October 1947. This was a great achievement and many other things happened in 1947. Interestingly a large number of secret agencies were created that year.

One thing is for sure is that the High Council were aware of these secret agencies and departments. And now they were more anxious to accelerate their plan.

With these entities implanted in the humans to help direct and stabilize things on Earth the plan can continue. With the new technology being learned the Council will have to accelerate things to stay ahead of the humans that might do things that could destroy the planet.

To start the meeting Ambrosia said to Leto "you need to read what is to happen next from the plan".

Leto read "it says that after a sufficient number of Avatars are in place, we are to start directing them to create an atmosphere that will bring about an awareness of global co-operation."

Aethusa asked "does it explain how we are to do this?"

Then Leto searched and said "it doesn't say."

Ambrosia said "well then we will have to study a bit more of the things the humans use for communication and infiltrate that for our own use. We will have to go slow with this and remember it won't start taking place until the Wayshowers are of age. Therefore their Guides will need to start preparing them for that time."

Hermes said "okay but don't forget we still have to keep their world from going into chaos or complete annihilation while we are teaching these children."

Dardanus said "right Hermes, that's why I think we should do what we did when they were of one mind and built that tower in Babel, we can just confound their language or do something similar."

Then Leto jumped up and said "Dardanus, you need to get on board with the plan. This time is different; we are preparing them to come home."

Ambrosia said "thank you Leto, now we will commission a group of elders to put together some ideas of how we will implement the plan at this juncture."

It was as clear as day, this dream, and Susan White thought *I must share this with Lucille*. So she phoned her and said "Lucille, we need to meet and talk about a dream I had last night."

Lucille replied "okay I'll stop by this afternoon." Before Lucille and little Paul would arrive Susan went over and over in her mind the dream that she had. All she could think about was, how vivid it was, and what her visitor had told her in the dream.

Knock, knock, Susan opens the door and says "why hello sister and my little Paul please come in" she was so happy. She made them some herbal tea, just like the kind in her dream and for some reason there were other little nuances that seemed important and the tea was one of them.

After two sips Lucille proclaimed "Okay, now tell me about

this dream you had?"

"Well, it was not only a vivid dream it has stayed with me all day. I dreamt that Paul was in his late 20's and a very successful doctor."

Her curiosity raised, Lucille then asked "Is there anything else?"

Susan sipping some more tea said "yes, he will graduate from Auburn just like you and Paul did." Okay so far Lucille was excited but that was her and Paul's plan all along. Susan knew that this wasn't anything new but in the dream she seen him as a doctor of Physics, and she didn't want to tell Lucille that yet.

Susan ended the conversation with "I know this is nothing new, but believe me this dream was wonderful".

Since Elizabeth has the Avatar from Maia in her and doesn't have a human Guide, she share's everything with Connor about Margaret. As she dreams about Margaret her visitor shares information about what will become of their little girl. This night was very special, the constellation of Taurus was visible, this was something that Elizabeth had no idea of until she was visited, and had her Spirit share her soul with her Avatar.

She had her first informative dream and in this dream she was seated with the Pleiadian High Council. She sat and listened to Councilor Ambrosia say. "We have a special guest tonight, this is Elizabeth Brown and her daughter Margaret is our Wayshower from Maia."

Elizabeth wakes up and feels like her Spirit is filled with hope and love for the future. Connor is back from getting some eggs for breakfast and says "good morning my sweet Angel".

She smiles and says "you are a Prince and will always have my heart. Now let's cook those eggs and eat." Before they finished breakfast she asked "can we talk about a dream I had last night?"

Connor replies "sure what's up Angel?"

Elizabeth smiles and said "I was taken to the Pleiadian High Council, I was then introduced to the Chiefs by Councilor Ambrosia, and then told of Margaret's future on Earth."

Connor was very interested. "Okay, please tell me everything."

"Well, mostly she is to become a writer and a politician".

"So where do we come in, in all this?"

"We are to read stories to her about the information I will be given."

"Wow! I'm all in just let me know what I can do to help" he then kissed her goodbye and went to work.

CHAPTER 3

From the Potsdam Conference of July – August 1945, the Allies decided to divide Korea, just like they divided Europe between east and west, only this would be north and south, and the 38th parallel became the political border. After the surrender of Japan, Korea was split, the north went to China, and the Soviet Union, and the south belonged to the UN. On June 25th, 1950 the North invaded the South, and the UN Security Council authorizes military force to repel the North's advance. Therefore the U.S. was back in another war, and I say the U.S. because it provided some 88% of the forces for the South. This was also the beginning of the Cold War.

With Margaret turning four and her brother William being two years old, Elizabeth had her hands full, and it goes without saying that she didn't want Connor to go and fight again. But Connor would be recalled and now fight in a regiment of the

Army's 7th Infantry Division at the Chosin Reservoir, from where he barely made it back!

Elizabeth went to bed this night with a very sad heart knowing that her husband was fighting in another war with all the tragedies that it will involve. While William and Margaret were asleep, she remembered some of the nightmares that Connor would wake up from, and this made her feel scared for him.

Later that night a bright light flashed in her room, as she woke, looked up, she noticed three figures that were dressed in all white, and were transparent as if they were made of light. She asked her Avatar "is this a dream?" There was no response, then when she awoke the next morning she recalled how they seemed to speak to her inside her heart, and they assured her that Connor was safe. All that day she would look at the beauty around her, and give her children all her love, and attention.

This time Dr. Paul Miller MD wasn't spared, in 1950 he was drafted into the Army as a surgeon at the rank of Captain. His practice was going so well that he had been so busy working, he and Lucille didn't try to have any more children. Shortly after Paul was drafted he was sent to Korea to help mend the soldiers in the war. Lucille's friend Susan tried to comfort her by helping her with Paul Jr. who was turning four. With Paul Jr's daddy having to leave to go off to war, Susan's children felt a special kinship with him.

The choppers keep coming in one after another bringing the wounded and Capt. Miller was doing the best he could to patch them up. "Bring that one over here, he looks to be the worst off and we need to get that bleeding stopped." He had been in Korea more than a month so this wasn't the first casualties he had seen. He went on to say "Where are these men coming from?"

One of the orderly's said "most of the men are from the Marines 1st Division and Army's 7th Infantry Division, they're coming from the battle of the Chosin Reservoir. Sir."

A few weeks later some soldiers went to that M.A.S.H unit to bring their men back, or on to their next duty station. One of the men that showed up was a Sgt. Connor Brown, and Capt. Miller was the duty officer the day he arrived to pick up his men. With a very crisp salute, Connor Brown said "Sgt. Brown reporting to pick up my men that were wounded sir."

Capt. Miller lowered his salute and said "Sgt. Brown I have two men to release to you, for duty." He then took their paperwork along with his men. Later that evening Capt. Miller would write home and mention meeting Sgt. Brown in his letter.

Dear Sweet Lucille,

I miss you so much. How is our son Paul doing? Do tell him that daddy is fine and I'll see him soon. The only thing I have to keep me from going crazy here is how busy we are patching up these poor men that keep coming in. Today I met with a Sgt. Brown that came here to pick up two of his men and bring them back to duty. This man cared for his men so much, that he would talk with them and would answer their questions that they had, even if it involved advice about their families back home...

Love Paul

While he was there he would meet and work with some very special people that would become his friends forever.

When Lucille read the letter to Susan she was given more insight about the meeting with Sgt. Brown. Susan had a dream or a visit some nights before and was told of some things that were to happen to the Miller's. Susan said "Lucille, I had a dream about Paul, and he would meet a man over there. This man was subordinate to him in some way, but he seems to command respect from Paul."

Lucille was thinking about what Susan said all the next day after their visit. She thought 'I wonder who this man was that my overly proud husband would give his respect to?' It's not that Paul wasn't respectful to others it's just that he was very proud of being a doctor and I think some cockiness rubbed off on him from his dad the Senator. So she just put that thought and the name of Sgt. Brown in her memory.

This conflict between the UN and the Communist countries cannot end well. At least that's the opinion of the High Council from the Pleiades. In their meeting Ambrosia asked Oenomaus "is our Avatar in place to help guide the Secretary General?" This is the first United Nations Secretary General Trygve Lie who was a socialist from an early age.

"Yes Your Grace she is a high level secretary in the planning department."

"What's this young lady's name?"

"Her name is Donna, your Grace."

"Leto, what's the first order of business on this current agenda?"

"Your Grace it would be to make sure another atomic bomb is not dropped, and to prevent a full scale world war."

"Oh that's all" snarled Dardanus.

Lie had been working tirelessly to prevent a war, but when North Korea invaded, and the Soviet Union supported them, he knew it would be hard to stop any retaliation by the Allied nations of the UN. The Secretary had several men on his Staff. One of them would get his information from his aides and one of those aides was dating Donna. Now Donna would share her dreams with her boyfriend, and they just happened to be very important answers to the current world problems.

Lycus offered "maybe if we can show them what the Earth looks like from space, this would inspire some leaders to work together and stop these wars?"

It was time for the optimist Darnanus to join in "the people already have some captured technology that's being used to create advanced electronics, and air travel. So how do we advance man into space travel, with the limited knowledge they already have?"

Ambrosia closed the session and said "this will be difficult with the Korean War in full swing. We should all come back with some ideas in tomorrow's session."

On the next day of the meeting, Leto stood up and proclaimed "all rise for our High Councilor Ambrosia."

Ambrosia said "please be seated and let the meeting begin." Leto read the minutes from the last meeting and the Chiefs gave their plans.

Oenomaus began "we on Sterope believe we should increase our Avatars in the UN to help steer these people away from total annihilation."

Then Ambrosia said "good idea now who's next?"

Hermes then stood up and read "we from Maia feel that part of the new plan should be to visit the seven top world leaders."

"And do what?" replied Dardanus.

Hermes read on further "Take them up into space and show them the need to co-operate with us."

"Now I like both plans." spoke Ambrosia.

Dardanus then said "I guess sending several fleets of our best warships are out of the question?"

Ambrosia laughed and that brought down the house. Leto thought *we sure needed that laughter*.

UN Secretary General Trygve Lie resigned in November 1952, he recommended Sweden's Dag Hammarskjöld to replace him.

Dwight D. Eisenhower became the new President of the United States. During the last year of the Korean conflict the U.S. was the main backer of troops and finances. Their new president was one of the two Supreme Allied Commanders in WWII, who knew firsthand the awfulness of war, and how industry profits from it. That said the armistice would be signed on July 1953, after only seven months into his Presidency.

It is now the time to let peace begin and start preparing the Wayshowers. Both Paul Miller and Connor Brown survived the war and would return home to their families.   The top seven world leaders will be given some galactic information and the future UN Secretary General's will have Avatars around them for guidance, and to help maintain the peace for some time to come.

CHAPTER 4

In 1947 Capt. Charles "Chuck" Yeager had broken the speed of sound flying the X-1 in the desert. A few months before Capt. Yeager did this, a UFO crashed down near Roswell, New Mexico. Only few years later these events were put on hold, until in 1953 when another bloody war is over, and there is peace again in most of the world.

There were some early humans that helped pave the way for space travel like; Konstantin Tsiolkovsky who back in 1880–1881 wrote a paper called "Theory of Gases". Unfortunately most of his work was not known outside of Russia. Another one was Robert H. Goddard who wrote a paper "A Method of Reaching Extreme Altitudes" in 1919. This led to liquid fuel V-2 rockets being developed in WWII by the German scientists. These German scientists were now working with the United States, and the Soviet Union scientists under the Operation Paper Clip program. This was set up after the war and it split them up between the two powerhouses.

The Council was in session again, this time after dodging a possible World War III, from the conflict in Korea, and the eagerness of then President Truman from dropping another atomic bomb. In this meeting Ambrosia said "Leto read from the plan".

"Yes Your Grace."

Before he could Dardanus said "is this the plan to get the two world powers involved in space travel?"

Ambrosia answered with "Yes it is, please read on Leto."

Leto read "It has been decided that a shadow government would give the USSR the technology they need to build and launch a satellite into space."

"Wouldn't this cause alarm in the U.S.?" asked Lycus.

"Yes it would, and the U.S. would turn their attention from the Cold War, and develop a Space agency to counter the Soviets."

Ambrosia closed the meeting by saying "we need to prepare the next group of Avatars with this information." They also felt it was time to give the people with Avatars a glimpse of what is to come in the future.

On their base, located on the dark side of the moon the elders prepared to carry out their plan. "A decision has been made to use the UN to protect governments around the world that have a different way of governing from each other." read elder Septary from Merope.

Then read elder Amerorth from Celaeno "this means the communists, capitalist, socialist, and all the other democracies are going to be used as a testing ground to determine the good and bad of each system."

"And what will that accomplish?" asked elder Derey from Sterope.

"This will mean that all human rights are protected." Amerorth said

"Then let's get the ships ready and send them to Earth." After this was said by Derey, all nodded in agreement.

Its 1957, the High Council have accomplished their goal of having the Soviet Union launch a satellite named Sputnik 1 into orbit around the Earth. A few years later in 1961, through rocket scientists Sergey Korolyov and Kerim Kerimov, they were instrumental in putting a Soviet cosmonaut Yuri Gagarin into space, which included putting the capsule into one orbit around mother Earth.

While the Millers were enjoying peace in the world. Little Paul was in school and his mom Lucille was working in dad's practice. Life couldn't be better for them. They had a nice home in Birmingham and a vacation home on the lake. On Wednesdays Paul would go play golf with some of his business and doctor friends, and Lucille would do the grocery shopping. She liked going during the week because little Paul was in school, and her friend Susan would almost always go with her. Both women loved buying fresh fruits, vegetables, and they were very health conscious, even before it was a thing.

Susan had another dream that seemed so real, she wasn't sure she woke up out of it, until she noticed her surroundings weren't the same as in the dream. Earth was so different, there were two moons, they were very close to the planet and they were colorful. She asked her visitor friend "what is this, is it the Earth or is it another planet?"

"Well, it's kind of both."

"Huh, it's kind of both."

"Yes, it's your new planet in the future and it comes out from the old one."

In her dream the Earth's gravity was nothing like it is now and she could move around wherever she imagined to go. The continents were at different levels of altitude, and the water was the most beautiful greenish blue you've ever seen. She would dive into the water that was on different levels in the air, and she could go through, under, or over it.

When she did dive into the water she would communicate with the creatures especially the dolphins. She didn't notice any humans just these light beings flying everywhere, and when she would come close to them, her body would feel a warmness that she would describe as pure love. She was excited about seeing Lucille and would need to share this with her probably on Wednesday during their 'tea time' after the shopping is done.

Wednesday couldn't get here fast enough for Susan, and she thought *now it's time to go shopping*. The girls are excited to see each other, well not as much as Susan. She is having a hard time containing herself about wanting to share this dream with her best friend. "Lucille what's new with you this last week?"

"A lot, Susan but you go first."

"Okay then, let me tell you about a dream I had."

As she is talking Lucille is mesmerized thinking about how beautiful the Earth was, and how wonderful it would be to live in such a place.

Lucille then says "that is beautiful and the new Earth sounds like a wonderful place. Little Paul is having some dreams where he has seen images of a big white polar bear at night beside his bed."

At first Susan didn't know what to say about this and then a thought came to her. "Have him drink some chamomile tea with you before he goes to sleep, encourage him to share his dreams with you, and to not be afraid."

"Thanks you are the best big sister I never had."

Paul and Lucille are working at their office planning their future, while little Paul is going to school. Now that is how normal their lives are on the outside, all the while Susan starts Lucille on a path of studying a lot of things that are frowned on by her church. They would visit the library, reading books about astrology, about dreams, and their meanings. Talking with his mom, Paul Jr. now 14, was starting find an interest in the meta-physical sciences, but he would tell his dad that he wants to be a medical doctor just like him.

Connor and William were up early this Saturday morning, the rain had come that night, and the moon before was right for planting. Then Connor said to William "can this place be any more beautiful?"

William said "I don't think it can dad."

They were getting the tractor loaded when they noticed some strange blue lights in the sky to the east. These were very much like the Northern Lights or Aurora Borealis clouds. Where they lived in Indiana, the location due east of them, would be Wright Patterson Air Force base.

Connor had read that the cargo plane which left Roswell in 1947, after the UFO crash, had travelled to Fort Worth, Texas, left there, and flew to Wright Patterson Air Force Base for good.

Elizabeth didn't understand the dream she had but, it was a beautiful one. The dream was very a very lucid one, so she didn't want to wake up. Again she was taken back to one of the Pleiades star clusters, where she then met a new Pleiadian. "Hello Elizabeth, my name is Aethusa and I am a chief from Alcyone."

Then Elizabeth put out her hand and said "nice to meet you, I see you already know who I am."

Aethusa replied with "oh, oh course I do, for you have a very important job to do."

Elizabeth was excited and asked "what would that be?"

Aethusa replied "Well since the Council can't travel to the Earth and put an end to all the wars, poverty, and hate that have been going on, we need to have Wayshowers do this instead. We have a plan, that will start sometime around 1965 with them becoming of age, and you are one of many that will guide them in doing that."

The next day Elizabeth started helping Margaret, who was now 14 years, old write down some of her poems. It seems her dreams were inspiring Margaret to write about them. Holding up the note pad she said "Mom, what about this one?

Our Beautiful Planet

Earth is a beautiful planet bright and blue.
A part of the galaxy that is so very new.

She gives her love to the animals that grew.
But the people have used her until now she is through.

Then some visitors came from far away.
Teaching the people to change and to live another way.

Margaret Brown 1960

At the time there was a lot of talk about UFO's, since the Roswell incident there were a lot more sightings. Connor described to Elizabeth and Margaret what he and William had seen in the sky to the east. They were all very receptive to things that are described as supernatural or meta-physical.

Elizabeth shared her dream with him and Margaret read her first poem. He was very happy to hear both and thought how blessed he was to have such a loving eclectic family. Margaret loved it when her mom would talk about the planets in the solar system and how they are thought to be Gods in Greek mythology. Also Margaret and her mom were starting to have very similar dreams.

John F Kennedy was our new President. He would be instrumental in getting the space race started... "... I believe that this nation should commit itself to achieving the goal, before this decade is out, of landing a man on the Moon and returning him safely to the Earth. No single space project in this period will be more impressive to mankind or more important for the long-range exploration of space; and none will be so difficult or expensive to accomplish." (Source Wikipedia)

CHAPTER 5

On October 14, 1962, CIA U-2 spy planes took photographs of intermediate-range ballistic missile sites being built in Cuba by the Soviets. The photos were shown to Kennedy on October 16; a consensus was reached that the missiles were offensive in nature and thus posed an immediate nuclear threat. (Source Wikipedia)

Not since the Korean conflict has the world been tested with a nuclear war. The Avatars will need to influence the leaders of the world to stop and think about the dangers a nuclear war would cause. Where several avatars like Donna, in the UN, they will be instrumental in bringing this situation to a peaceful resolution.

An agreement was reached between presidents Kennedy and Khrushchev, in which the United Nations was to verify that all USSR weapons would be removed from Cuba, and secretly the U.S. would remove their Jupiter missiles from Turkey. In 1963

President Kennedy was assassinated.

The High Council did not go into session this time around, but instead they went on high alert just in case. They wanted to see how well the Avatars would do their jobs. They performed perfectly by stopping a war, and turning both sides back to focus on their space programs.

Paul had become quite interested in the books his mom would bring home, especially the ones dealing with metaphysics. He found an interest in the great philosophers like Plato and Socrates', but he did tend to think more about this from a science standpoint. They were doing their weekly reading at the library when Lucille started asking Susan some questions about Paul's interest in Physics. "Susan I have a question."

Susan put her book down and moved her eyes above her glasses and said "yes."

"Paul has been reading some of my books on philosophy, and he seems to be finished with that. He has asked some scientific questions about what we are made of."

Susan replied with "I would suggest he start with Max Planck he was the originator of the quantum theory."

"Great, I'll tell him."

It was time for dinner at the Miller home and dad was being quiet this night until Lucille spoke. She looked at her son and said "Paul I was talking with Susan today at the library and she suggested you do some research on a scientist named Max Planck."

Paul asked his mom "Who is he?"

"He was the originator of the quantum theory."

Then dad said "I've heard of him, he wrote about atomic and sub-atomic scaled particles."

Paul Jr. replied "really dad, now that's cool."

This was a gateway for Paul Jr. to learn about energy and matter and how we as humans are all made from this. He would study about Max Planck and, of course Albert Einstein, which helped prepare him for his venture to college.

On the farm in Indiana the Browns have just planted their crops. "Dad let's go shoot some hoops" said William.

"Sure we've got some extra time before dinner." Off they went doing what Hoosiers do best and that's shoot basketball.

Margaret and her mom were busy talking about some poems she wrote. She said "mom this one was an inspiration about your dreams of being a leader in another galaxy."

"Then please read it to me, my dear."

Margaret then opened up her note pad and read.

Councilor Ambrosia

I have a great desire to lead,
people who are of my own seed.

My mission is to guide them with Love
and this is the truth I know from above.

Teach them what is so clear,
to allow our Love to replace all fear.

Margaret Brown 1962

Elizabeth then said "that is very beautiful dear."

As the days went by, Elizabeth and Margaret would spend a lot of time together, with mom telling her about her dreams, and then Margaret writing down poems about them. This was part of the plan from the High Council, to take Elizabeth to places in her dreams and then have Margaret write them into poems.

Margaret Brown and Paul Miller Jr. will be graduating from high school soon, then going to college to carry their gifts, talents, ideas, thoughts, and love to blend with other Wayshowers in the world with them.

Paul was prepared to go to medical school just like his dad. His mom and Susan knew that in his heart he was very interested in the science of quantum theory. One thing about Paul was he is a very grateful young man and when something catches his attraction he will follow or search it out to the ninth degree.

Susan was instrumental in helping Lucille guide this young Wayshower named Paul, and to teach him in the ways of his ancestors the Pleiadians from Celaeno. She never could tell him who he was, and she could only use her dreams to educate his mother, so she would use this knowledge to prepare him for when that day came.

One night alone in his room after a tough day in medical school he said something out loud to himself that would set him on a path of enlightenment. He said "here I am, in this physical body but I know that I am made of pure light energy". Then after some quiet meditation he said "God, if you can hear me, please guide me in the direction you would want me to go."

That night Paul would be taken somewhere in his dreams he had never been before, at least not in this body. "Wow, where am I?" he said while dreaming. Then he met a different looking creature but felt in his heart that he knew him before.

This strange looking Pleiadian said "hello I am a Guide to your mother's friend Susan and I am from this planet you are now visiting".

Paul gulped knowing he was dreaming, but he had control over his body in this dream, and said "okay, what does this have to do with me?"

The visitor said "well, I am now your Guide and we are both from this planet called Celaeno."

He had to ask his Guide "I've been here before; I guess that's why it seems so familiar, right?" Then the morning came and Paul was back in his body and then awoke.

Class wasn't easy for him that day, for all he could think about was the dream. He was sitting in class and thought *what was that dream about and can I go back there tonight?* Those answers were all that he wanted to know that day, and thankfully it was a short day in school.

Now a lot of the things that he had learned from his mom and Susan seemed to make more sense. He is now on the path of realizing who he was, and what his mission is on this planet called Earth. Therefore he knew that he would have help along the way.

Susan would no longer have her dreams that she would share with Lucille. This made her sad but when she watched Paul grow to become the Wayshower he is, it made it all worthwhile.

It's Richmond, IN, in 1965, and mommy's little girl is looking to go off to college. "Margaret, what do think of this one?" her mom said.

She put down her brochure of one of many school prospects and said "which one mom?"

Elizabeth wanted her to go to a local college, so she would be close to home. "How about Miami University" Elizabeth said.

Margaret replied "I don't know mom I've got several offers and I'd like to see some new places."

Elizabeth then said "well give me a list of a few that you like, and we can pick one out."

"Okay mom, I love you."

She looked at her daughter and said "you are so very special to me, I love you too."

That night Elizabeth had a very puzzling dream. She was taken back to the High Council, but this time she wasn't a visitor. "What am I doing here and where is my Guide?" she said.

Ambrosia answered her and said "Elizabeth you are an elder from Maia and your presence is needed back on the council. Your Guide was you all along."

She felt very cold because she knew what this would mean, and she didn't think she was ready. "So, I'm back on the council tonight to help out with something, and my Guide and I are one again?" she said.

The doctors were puzzled because she was very healthy, so they just listed her death as, *of natural causes*. This was a very sad day for the Brown family. They weren't sure they could go on without Elizabeth.

Connor went off alone into the woods and asked God "why did you take her from me, and our children? Don't you know how much we love and need her?" He then thought from his heart *how did I survive two wars and then have my wife taken from me in her sleep?* No answer came back audibly but after many a tear, Connor was given the strength to carry on.

Margaret stayed at home and postponed college for a year, just to make sure her dad, and brother would be okay. After several months passed she had a dream that would change her life forever. "Mom is that you?" she said in her dream.

"Yes dear it's me" replied Elizabeth, who now was called Terames from her native planet of Maia.

Margaret was so excited to see and talk with her, she said "mom I miss you so much. What happened, why did you die?"

Terames answered her "my dear we don't die we just move on to our next life, or back to where we are from. Now dear I want you to go off to college, your dad and brother will be fine."

She woke up and decided where she would go to school. In the fall of that year she would go to Montgomery, Alabama, and study at Auburn University.

The High Council now back in session, where they have some very important business to attend to.

"Leto, we need to officially welcome a fellow Pleiadian back from Earth." said Ambrosia with a very welcoming smile.

"Yes your Grace, please welcome Terames an elder from the planet Maia." The whole assembly went wild with applause.

"Now back to business" said Ambrosia.

Leto read from the latest update of the Plan "the final ships have delivered their last Wayshowers to Earth. We now have exactly 144,000 of them scattered throughout the planet."

"That is wonderful news, what's next?" asked Aethusa.

Leto then read the next part "we are to start them on their missions to change the world and prepare the way for their return home."

Dardanus said "we will need to map their futures on Earth and see that they receive the support they need."

"Right and we will need to make them aware of The Secret. So let's close our business and come back with our plans.

Yes Hermes, you have something to add?" said Ambrosia

"I do, your Grace, my elder Terames would like to ask if it's possible to be the Guide of her daughter Margaret on Earth."

Ambrosia looked at Terames and said "of course it would my dear, it would be our honor."

CHAPTER 6

A deferment from the Draft is what Paul was granted. Now that he started college, he was not interested in going to war, so college suited him just fine. He is just like his dad was back then, always having fun. In one class Paul said "Mr. Green are you sure that those photons can't travel faster than light?" He did have some fun in school, but soon his dreams were going to make school look like chumps play.

This night wasn't any different than any other one, so before he would go to sleep, he would ask his new Guide to contact him. *Yes, I'm back* was all Paul could think while dreaming. He then said "Mr. Guide, I'm ready for some information."

"Good, we have a lot to do, but first we are going tp go on a little trip."

As Paul's body was deep in sleep his Spirit was lifted and travelled up into space. This mode of travel happened so fast that he said "where are we?"

"We are on the dark side of the moon."

"The dark side of the moon, how cool! What is that, a base?"

"Yes it's our moon base from the Pleiades."

The next thing Paul knew was that his alarm went off. He said "darn, back to school."

School was very important to Paul, even though he was heavily interested in quantum theory, he still had to get his biology work done, and turned in. "Miss Carter, did you say this paper would be due in two weeks?"

"Ha, ha, Mr. Miller it is due on Monday."

"Okay, thank you" He then smiled at her, picked up his books, and headed for his next class.

While in his next class, which was algebra he started thinking about the trip he took the night before. *Did I really go to the other side of the moon, and should I believe these dreams are real?*

That evening he asked his mom. "Mom, would you have some tea with me before retiring to bed?"

"Sure son, I have some good herbal tea, so we can just sit, relax, and concentrate on our dreams tonight." His mom would say "tea, it works every time it's tried." Also this was one of the things Susan taught her to do.

Margaret was still getting settled in when she met her new roommate. "Hello my name is Margaret Brown" she said as she reached out her hand.

"Glad to meet you, you are my new roomie and my name is Tammy Jones." Tammy helped Margaret get unpacked and asked "do you want to go for pizza tonight?"

Margaret smiled and said "sure why not, that bus ride was long. I will need to call my dad and little brother first."

"What about your mom?"

Margaret could feel her mom inside her heart, and said "my mom is always with me." Tammy was speechless, but had a really good positive feeling about what she heard.

"Margaret what are you going to major in?"

"Well, I write a lot of poems about life and the universe so literature is certainly in there." then she took another sip of her water and said "probably civics or political science, I've always been interested in government, how about your major?"

Tammy thought *that's interesting*. "I'm going to nursing school. My mom's a nurse and my dad is a business man."

Margaret shrugged her shoulders and said "I guess we won't have many, if any classes together then."

She really missed her mom and this night she was with her. "Mom, how have you been?"

"Fine dear, everything is going as planned. Now that you are going to college we have some work to do."

"What would that be? I do have plenty of school work ahead."

Terames then assured her and said "don't worry about school, your goal is to do what feels right in your soul, and I will help you achieve it."

"How will you do this, by giving me the answers for my tests?"

"No, silly girl the whole universe is there to help you. I will guide you with dreams, and people will come into your life to help you along the way."

She then woke up to her alarm and went off to her first day of class. Once there she noticed the word *university* and thought about what her mom told her *the whole universe is there to help you.* She sighed and said under her breath *thank you mom for being here at this (universe) university to help me.* She jotted down a poem in her notebook.

Universal Love

The universe is here as our guide,
An enormous force, that's on our side.

If we feel lost and are in dismay,
It will be there to help us find our way.

Margaret Brown 1966

At the next High Council meeting it was Hermes turn to give his report. He then said "Your Grace, I would like to update the Council on the progress of Terames' daughter Margaret."

Ambrosia smiled looking at Terames "please do Chief Hermes."

"Yes Your Grace, Margaret is enrolled in college, where she has majored in political science, with her minor being in literature. This is just as planned as she continues to write poems about her dreams."

"Thank you Hermes, how are her dreams coming along?"

Hermes replied after looking at Terames "she is doing well your Grace, she is very happy knowing her mother is with her at all times."

There were many meetings of the council, and in one of them Paul Miller was mentioned. "Please give your report Chief Lycus" announced Leto.

"Thank you Leto, I report that Paul Miller has met his new Guide, who now knows that his mom's friend Susan was instructed by this same Guide. Paul is enrolled in the medical program at Auburn University, which is his parents' alma mater."

Ambrosia said "excellent, how is his progress so far?"

"Very well Your Grace he is excited about his dreams and is eager to be taught."

Leto then knew it was time to end the meeting so the next step in the Plan was read "we are to focus them on their gifts, and make sure there are Avatars in place to facilitate them along on their path.

Ambrosia said "thank you all, meeting adjourned."

Paul wanted to learn more about the base on the moon. While sitting in class trying to stay focused, all he could think was *every time I go to sleep I'm visited by my Guide. I would be taken somewhere or shown something new. Then I would wake up and forgot to ask about the moon base.* This troubled him so much that he devised a plan to make sure he would ask this question the next time around.

Meta-physical stores were starting to pop-up in the area of the campus and Paul thought *maybe I can find a way of tapping into these dreams there?*

"Hello may I help you?" said this beautiful older lady.

Paul turned around and noticed she was speaking to him. "Yes mam, you may, my name is Paul Miller and I would like to talk to you about dreams."

"My name is Dorothy Crane and this is my store. What would you like to know about your dreams?"

"Well, I've been having these certain lucid ones for a while now, and there is this what I call a visitor in my dreams. The visitor is from the planet Celaeno, and he used to be my mom's best friend's Guide, and he is now mine."

She quickly put up her hand and said "say no more, we need to talk in private about this." Paul was taken back, so they both set a date to meet again the next day.

That night in his dreams he was again taken to the moon base. "Okay visitor what will I learn tonight?"

"Mr. Miller, you don't know yet who you are, but I will begin to tell you tonight."

"First off you never gave me your name, secondly today I met someone at a meta-physical store who seemed to want to tell me something about my dreams."

"Paul you can call me Ringo, isn't that the name of the drummer of the Beatles band that you like? This lady named Dorothy you met was put there to meet Wayshowers like yourself. She is an Avatar from the planet Merope and she will help you in this physical plane of existence."

"I never told you her name and that sure is a lot of info. Please tell me what a Wayshower is?" He then he woke up.

He went back to visit Dorothy the very next day. She was a kind soul and ready to help Paul understand his dreams. "Mrs. Crane I had another dream last night"

"Okay young Paul you can tell me what your visitor from the planet Celaeno said?"

"My visitor is called Ringo, when I told him about you he said that you are an Avatar, from the planet Merope, and that you will help me understand my dreams. He also knew your name!"

She then unfolded her arms and lifted them up and said "Ambrosia your Grace, and Chief Lycus, I thank you for giving me this opportunity to help this Wayshower from Celaeno. I will give my reports to Sinon once a week." For the next three years she helped young Paul understand who he is.

Dr. Martin Luther King Jr. and Robert "Bobby" Kennedy have been shot and killed. The Vietnam War is in full swing, and a new administration has been elected in Washington, promising to end the war. The young people are taking action and half a million meet in a place called Woodstock, New York for a concert and celebration.

"Jimi Hendrix, Crosby, Stills, Nash, and Young, plus many more artists this should be fun" said Tammy during lunch with her friends in medical school.

Paul was at the next table and heard Tammy talk. "What is she talking about?" he asked one of his friends.

Greg replied "she's talking about a big three day concert in upper state New York, to protest the war."

"Cool, I'd like to go there" said Paul.

Margaret had heard about this concert too, when she did, she thought about her dreams, and all that she had been told by her mom and Ambrosia. After all she was told that, she was a Wayshower, and that she was here to help the people on this planet move to a higher level of consciousness. So while sitting in her room she reflected on what she had learned so far. Then she wrote a poem to remember what she was taught.

The Wayshower

A generation of visitors from very far,
Will awake and learn who they are.

Their purpose is as complex as history;
Guides have come to teach them this mystery.

For the day will come to be shown.
All that we the Masters have known.

It is with honor to teach some
of the people this Secret to come.

What is The Secret you say?
It is to live your life in a better way.

What is this way and has it been shown?
Yes, by the Masters from the throne.

Are we to learn only from Kings?
Yes, to Love and cause our Hearts to sing.

Margret Brown 1969

When she read this to her friend, Tammy looked at her and said "where do you get this from?"

"I don't know, maybe from my mom in my dreams."

Later that Saturday the girls decided to ride into town to get a bite to eat. Tammy asked Margaret "why don't you eat meat?"

"I'm not really sure, I used to but since my mom left I just stopped. I do like seafood and lots of pasta." she said trying not to notice the smell of Tammy's burger.

"Okay, no problem just curious. Hey did you hear about the concert in New York State?" Tammy said after moving her burger off to the side.

"Yes, I did hear about it and one of my favorite singers will be there."

"Well, who is it?"

"Oh I'm sorry, it's Joan Baez!"

Later that evening on the phone with her dad, Margaret was listening to him talk about Catherine (Margo) O'Donnell, who was a young Irish country singer that he liked listening too. Her dad wanted to start calling her Margo so she agreed to make Margo her nickname and she liked it.

The girls were back in school and they were to meet for dinner. Tammy had a late lab class therefore Margo offered to eat a late dinner with her. Margo had often thought of Tammy as her twin sister, and they were only a few months apart in age.

At the restaurant Tammy grabbed Margo's hand and said "go with us to the Woodstock concert."

"Who are you going with?"

"A bunch of us in medical school are going. We are renting a bus because our group right now is about 20 or so." Tammy then picked up her menu.

Margo thought *well I don't know these people but I'll be with Tammy so why not.* "I'll have the cod and brown rice with a salad."

Tammy looked up from her menu and noticed the waitress "oops sorry, I'll have the alfredo and a salad."

"So you'll have the chicken alfredo and a salad?"

Tammy then said "no, just the pasta, no chicken."

Margo smiled and told Tammy "I would love to go to the concert with you and your friends."

"We have to stop these young people from taking drugs" said Ambrosia.

"Yes your Grace, we need to keep them in the herbal community, and not ingest those chemically created drugs" replied Oenomaus.

"I've noticed that we are losing some of our Wayshowers to the war and these drugs" said Dardanus.

Ambrosia looked at Leto and said "what are we to do? The number is supposed to be 144,000."

"Yes Your Grace it says right here that; when one is lost during the 70 year period they are to be replaced by another of the same age from their Pleiadian group."

Sinon stood up and said "the Plan is starting to really take form."

"Yes, it's all written here" replied Leto.

Lacedaemon stood up and said "we will need to send a message to our moon base, that the Wayshowers are to learn who they are, and to start their missions."

"Good point Lacedaemon, we need to get our teams together to go there, and start this phase of the Plan" replied Ambrosia.

Then after things settled down, Ambrosia asked the Chiefs for an update. "Chiefs give your report."

Lycus was ready and said "Paul Miller is on schedule, he

has met with Dorothy Crane who is one of his Avatars. He will learn about his dreams from her and she will introduce him to other people on his path."

When Hermes stood up Terames was right there when Hermes said "our Wayshowers are moving on to their next level your Grace."

Looking over at Terames, Ambrosia then asked Hermes "how is Margaret doing?"

"Your Grace she is now being called Margo and she is right on track."

"Excellent, do you have any Avatars lined up to help her?"

"We do your Grace, they are in place."

Bethel, New York is about a thousand miles away. There are 27 people on the bus and it will take about three days to get there. Margo will get to know them all along the way.

CHAPTER 7

On the bus for the trip to New York State, where there is a big concert! Tammy made sure she introduced Margo to everyone on the bus, that's because Margo wasn't part of the medical college at Auburn. "Hello Sharon, this is my roomie Margo Brown."

Sharon reached out her hand and said "nice to meet you, I haven't seen you in medical school?"

"Nice to meet you, but I'm not in medical, my major is in political science, with a minor in literature." After meeting everyone the girls went back to their seats.

Two days later, and still riding the bus, but with only 30 miles to go. "That was a long ride" exclaimed Tammy to Margo.

"Yes it was" she said to Tammy.

"What do you think of the medical students, any future doctors you might want to meet?"

Margo smiled "I'm not really looking to meet anyone right

now so, I guess not thinking about any of them."

"That's too bad."

Paul Miller said "okay everyone we need to get in line and buy tickets." Tammy knew him briefly, but they never really talked much. They had a few classes together over the last few years.

Now Margo was excited and said to Tammy "look, at the schedule Joan Baez is playing tonight!"

"Great it looks like she's playing last after Arlo Guthrie. I just love Alice's Restaurant."

Then Greg said "Let's stay with the group ladies, wouldn't want anything to happen to you."

Later that evening their group became a little concerned about all the drugs that were being used. They didn't mind some alcohol or pot, but being in medical school they were well aware of the dangers that some drugs have.

One of the fellow attendee's said "hello ladies how about doing a snort with me and my buddies?"

Margo looked at him, smiled, and then said "no thank you, we are fine."

He then grabbed her by the arm, and said "I guess we aren't good enough for you and your friend?"

Tammy then yelled "you let go of her!"

Paul and Greg noticed the commotion, and they walked over there. Greg said "I would advise you to let her go and just move on pal." Now Greg not only was a football player, but he played on the offensive line, therefore he wasn't a pushover.

The men looked at Paul and Greg, then noticed the group behind them, and then one said "okay guys let's leave these losers alone."

—

So just like everything in life "The show must go on" and it did. The music was great! There were a lot of young people, and some older ones too, all enjoyed the whole atmosphere. Later that evening, of the first day, Paul and Greg were walking around and heard Margo say "there she is, there she is!"

Paul looked up, all around, and then at the schedule, and said "ah that's Joan Baez going on stage."

Margo not only liked Joan's music, but she was with her on the political issues of the day. A lot of the people there were of the same belief also. She was talking to her friend Tammy and asked her "isn't she great!"

Tammy looked at Joan on stage and said "her music is good but, I don't know, she's very good, I wouldn't say great."

Margo put her hand on Tammy's left shoulder and said "No, no, no, I like her music, but I mean the fact that she has gotten out there politically, and she's marched with the other's, who are demanding equal rights."

Then Paul and Greg overheard Tammy's reply "I guess she is great."

"Oh yes! She was there with us, at the 1965 Selma to Montgomery march with Dr. Martin Luther King Jr. for voting rights." Margo said very excitedly.

"Wow I didn't know that, and you were ther too?" was Tammy's answer and question.

"Yes we had a group go from our politics class."

After talking with Dorothy Crane during the last few years, a lot of what she had said started to make sense to Paul. After the shows were over that first day, it was time to crash. Their group had brought some tents and they made a little camp by their bus.

Later they created a circle around the campfire, where they all reflected on the events of the day. As the time went by, several in the group turned in for the night, which had left Paul, Greg, Tammy, and Margo remaining there with a few others talking.

In the quiet, of the night air, Greg said "do any of you know anyone that is over in Vietnam?"

Margo said to Greg "yes, my brother William signed up a couple of years ago."

Paul remembering that his dad was drafted into the Korean conflict, asked her "why did he volunteer?"

"Well my dad was drafted in WWII, where he fought in the Pacific. He was later recalled into service for the Korean conflict. He was in the infantry both times, and didn't like having to kill other people, or to see his friends die around him."

Paul did not understand where this was going, so he put up his hand, and said "wait, then why would your brother volunteer for war?"

Being a gentle soul, she then said "dear Paul my dad convinced him to enlist, that way he could pick the job he would have while over there."

Looking very pleased, Paul said "ah that makes perfect sense. Then what is he doing over there?"

Margo smiled at him and said "he is in the Air Force, making runways for the fighter jets." This was a very important encounter for these two. That evening something happened to them that couldn't be anything less than cosmic.

In their tent Paul looked over at his friend and said "Greg, I didn't smoke any pot today but just smelling it sure does relax you."

"Yea man, you are so right. I feel like I'm on cloud nine" then Greg's head slammed into his big, white, and fluffy pillow.

In another tent Margo and Tammy couldn't get to sleep, they would talk about the day's activities, and compare notes on some of the young doctors in the group.

Then later Margo looked at her friend, and said "girl my thoughts are drifting so far away, I had better go to sleep. I think my Spirit wants to leave this body, and go somewhere else."

Tammy said in a very tired voice "girlfriend you are somewhere else."

Paul said in his dream "Ringo, this isn't the moon base, where are we?"

"You are to meet the High Council of the Pleiades tonight."

Then as Paul entered the big chamber he heard someone speak. He looked over to hear Ambrosia say "welcome Paul Miller you are one of our guests this evening."

"Thank you, Your Grace. May I ask who you are?"

"Why sure, my name is Ambrosia, and you were correct in referring to me as Your Grace, because I sit as the High Councilor of the Pleiades."

Paul felt honored, he also very distant from his home planet Earth.

Margo said in her dream "mom I've felt your presence with me throughout this glorious day" when her mom (Terames) made herself known.

Terames then grabbed her hand and said "we must go to the Council tonight there is someone there for you to meet."

She took a deep breath, literally, and said "who?"

Terames then said on their way "you'll see soon enough."

They opened the chamber doors, then after they greeted

Councilor Ambrosia, Margo couldn't believe her eyes, and looking at this new visitor, she said "Paul, Paul Miller, what are you doing here? Mom is this for real or just part of my dream?"

Terames had to smile and chuckle at her daughter's paradoxical question. "Dear this is a dream and one that is real in the Spirit world."

Not being able to control her excitement "is he conscious in my dream, or just my creation?"

Paul said to Margo "Enough of this, what do you mean am I conscious? I'm right here aren't I? Now what are you doing in my dreams?"

Margo laughed and said "drams, so this isn't the only one?"

Ambrosia then spoke "children your Spirits are together in this dream."

They both looked at each other and said in unison "DEEP!"

Paul said "let's get on with it then. Margo, is Terames your Guide, I heard you call her mom?"

She smiled and replied "yes Paul, she is both. She crossed over about a year before I started college. She was an Avatar and also a mom on this earth, and now she is my Guide."

Feeling a deep love for her, Paul said with tears "that is so tragic and so beautiful. I don't know what else to say."

"I know she asked to be my Guide. Then several months later after her passing she visited me one night, and started me on this path. Who is your Guide?"

Paul looked at Ringo, and then laughed "he calls himself Ringo. Ringo was my mom's best friends Guide, but had no name and chose this one for me after my favorite drummer, weird huh?"

Before her friend Tammy would wake up, she wrote a poem about her dream, last night.

Choosing Love

This current realm is made up of two spheres,
one is Love and the other one is fear.

We choose Love to pattern our lives by,
to be free as a bird that just loves to fly.

The path we choose is never set in stone,
we being a Spirit that is destined to roam.

The day will come when you meet your twin-flame,
this is an important part of our Earthly game.

But don't be sad if this person isn't here yet,
they are out there and just waiting to be met.

Margo Brown 1969

When she woke the next morning, she looked over at Tammy, and said "good morning, what a beautiful day." Margo was so happy to learn, that she wasn't the only one, to have these dreams.

Tammy was getting her shoes on and said, "we need to get dressed, because breakfast needs to be prepared, and we have to pitch-in."

"Tammy you are so right, I'll be ready in two shakes" She said as she stood up.

Paul and Greg were already out getting the equipment ready to cook, some eggs, and bacon. While placing the thick bacon on the pan, Paul said to Greg "man that smell would have woke me up last night."

Greg taking a whiff said "yea man, love me some bacon."

The guys decided to cook while the girls got ready.

Paul wanted to talk with Margo about their dream last night, but he barely knew her, so he didn't know what to say. After breakfast he spotted her, over by the stage, talking with one of the roadies. He cleared his throat, and said "good morning Margo. Did you sleep well last night?"

Margo turned around and said "Paul, good morning to you too, and yes I did. I had an interesting dream last night."

"Me too" he said under his breath. He then got nervous and said "well good talking with you, I gotta go bye."

All through the day, both Paul and Margo knew they needed to talk with each other. Paul was making plans on how he would create the opportunity to talk with her. Margo would imagine what it would be like to discuss the High Council, and the Plan of the Pleiadians with him. They both wanted to find a way of talking about this soon.

He wasn't trying to avoid her, but he didn't want to be too anxious either. That afternoon Paul said this to his friend, "Greg, I need your help."

Greg was listening to the music and didn't hear him. Paul grabbed his arm and moved him back away so they could talk. "What's up Paul?"

"I really like Margo and I can't seem to get up the courage to talk with her."

Greg then laughed and said "You not having courage,

that's a new one."

Paul knew this was lame, but had to use the word "like" instead of the truth.

"Okay then what do you want me to do to help?"

It wasn't a difficult task for Greg to do, he liked Tammy anyway. So as Greg sees her by the bus with Margo, he says to her "Tammy do you have a minute? I would like to talk with you about something." he said walking towards her.

Tammy looked at him and thought *this should be interesting* and said "sure."

He walked her over to a little spot on the hill, where he told her about Paul's desire to talk with Margo.

There she is, thought Paul, *and times a wasting.* He soon after several inner attempts broke the silence, with "hello Margo how is your day?"

"Doing fine Paul, yourself?" Was all she said, but she wanted to say something else.

Paul then made his move, "can we go somewhere quiet and talk?"

Margo wanting to do this too said "you bet we can."

Expecting her to look at him puzzled, he said, "Margo, sure we don't know each other that well, but I had a very strange dream last night, and it involved you."

She then grabbed both of his hands, looked him in the eyes, and said "so, I in your dream?"

He did all he could to control his fear and excitement, and quickly said "yes, you were!"

They spent the rest of the afternoon together, talking about their dreams, and being amazed at how perfectly the same they were in all aspects. Walking back to the group camp area they decided to go back and see their friends. Later in the evening they were both with their friends, but tried not to reveal their dreams to them.

Before Greg and Paul had turned in for the night, Greg asked him "did you talk to her? I can't tell if you did from your expression."

Paul took a breath and collected his thoughts before he answered with "yes, I said hello and asked her about the concert. We spent most of the day just walking around and getting to know each other.

How about you and Tammy, did you two hit it off?"

"No, we talked mostly about you and Margo and then she had to leave."

The girls were talking about the guys and Tammy asked Margo "did Paul talk with you today?"

Margo thought for a second *how did she know that* then she smiled, and said "why yes, he did, I suppose you, and Greg were talking it up."

Tammy laughed "okay, okay it was a set-up, Paul wanted to get to know you."

Margo then picked up her notebook, and said "well he was successful, because we not only talked all day, we are going to spend most of tomorrow together."

"Wow, I guess the feeling is mutual, and I can see you want to write, so goodnight girl."

Waking up with her notebook in hand she said to herself *hum no dream last night?* So she thinks about the day spent talking with Paul. She thinks about how these two have something very different in common, then maybe anyone else does. She also reflects on what a gentleman he is, how handsome, and that she even starts adding Miller to her name. Laughing to herself she decides to write a poem, trying to capture her feelings in this moment.

Someone

Emotions in our lives are the fuel of leaving,
the results of lessons of Love, and of grieving.

Hold true young Wayshower your life is set,
therefore the goal is to believe in all to be let.

If one comes along on this same path,
know that we are few when you do the math.

To share this walk with another makes it complete,
seeing this does bind us as one, and not to compete.

Life, Love, and faith are not just words to relate,
these words work with our thoughts in order to create.

Margo Brown 1969

CHAPTER 8

Paul did have a dream the next night, and woke up thinking about it. He thought *maybe I should write some of this down?*

I was taken to the dark side of the moon, and in this Pleiadian base I was shown a lot of fascinating things. First, I was shown the current solar system, and how it operates with a mathematical equation that would cause the best mathematicians to collapse. Then I was shown how we were made out of Atoms and coded with DNA. This dream is hard to explain because I think some of this isn't even known to man yet."

Paul Miller 1969

They had told their friends that, this day was to be spent together, and it was the third day, (sounds like something from the book of Genesis). Paul sat down at the table with Margo and Tammy, and said "good morning ladies, you both look beautiful today." He loved giving compliments, and this was one of the many secrets to life that Dorothy had taught him.

Tammy just giggled and said "Mr. Miller you are such a gentleman."

He bowed to her, and said "thank you my lady." Margo just loved the way he would flirt with people.

Breakfast is over and the two Wayshowers are off talking, and feeling the oneness that comes from their other world. Margo asks him "Paul did you travel in your dreams last night?"

Paul gently grabs Margo's hand and said "yes, I went to the moon base, where I was shown a lot of knowledge about the universe. Did you have a dream too?"

She sighed and said "no, I feel asleep with my notebook in my hand, I then woke up to see the Sun coming over the hills, which inspired me to write another poem. Now, tell me about this, knowledge about the universe?"

"I know, it does sound funny, it was mostly about the planets, and the math equations that are used to keep them in orbit. Also some information about how our bodies are created with Atoms and DNA. So you write poems? I would love to read them sometime."

"Okay, we have a lot to talk about don't we?"

The day was spent mostly just walking and talking. Occasionally an entertainer would sing something they liked, they would stop to listen, rest, hydrate, and enjoy. "My brother is coming home in October, I'm planning on going home to see him, and my dad" she said.

He turned towards her and asked "can I drive you there?"

She said with a happy heart "I would really love you to do that." Being so close he leaned a little forward and gave her a very soft kiss.

Later that evening, Greg asked Paul "do you want to pack tonight or in the morning?"

"I'm not sure, what time we are leaving."

"Right after breakfast I think."

Paul thought and then said "let's do it tonight, I'm not too tired and I'm sure we will have plenty else to do in the morning." They packed up their stuff, then went to sleep.

In the girls tent Margo couldn't hide her feelings and Tammy was eager to explore them. "What happened today, you look so happy?"

Margo crossed her hands over her heart "he kissed me." She knew that telling Tammy this, would keep her mind too busy to ask questions about what she, and Paul talked about that day.

"I don't see you holding your notebook, are you not going to write tonight?" Margo smiled and said "no, I'm too tired, goodnight."

They were both taken to the High Council this night. Terames and Ringo both conversed about their two Wayshowers. She asked "Ringo, how is Paul coming along with getting to know my Margo?"

Ringo looked at her and said "just fine, he really likes her and they both seem happy together."

Paul then asked Ringo "sounds like you two have a lot to talk about. I would like to spend my time with Margo."

Terames looked at Ringo and then Paul and said "no, you two are here tonight to be given some instructions from your Chiefs and the High Councilor."

Leto proclaimed "all rise for your High Councilor Ambrosia."

Ambrosia then walked in, sat down and said "please be seated."

Hermes then spoke and said "Your Grace, Lycus and I have consulted with Terames and Ringo about our two Wayshowers. We have brought them here to the council to receive instructions from you."

Ambrosia stood up and said "thank you both, but first give your reports."

Now it was Lycus' turn to speak "Your Grace, Paul Miller is doing fine, he has met with Margo Brown as you know, and the two are growing together in their knowledge. Also he is using a lot of what Dorothy Crane has taught him, and is learning through his dreams with Ringo."

"Thank you, you're next Hermes"

"Thank you, Your Grace, Margo has met Paul Miller as all already know. She has been writing more and more poems, and is on track to include some of Paul's dreams also."

The two Wayshowers were given some other information, but the main jest of it all is, that they are to work closely together. This won't be hard to do, because they also have an attraction for one another.

The driver said "okay people we are leaving in 30 minutes, so be on the bus before then." They would take turns driving the bus, right now there was total confusion for all, but for Paul, and Margo they seemed to be unaffected by their surroundings.

They decided to sit together, even though it did bring a sense of amusement to Tammy, but Greg didn't give it much thought. "Well I see you are going to sit with Paul" Tammy said to Margo.

"Tammy, we have a lot in common and we want to spend

the ride getting to know each other better." It seemed that when Margo would explain things to Tammy, she would just accept it and move on.

"Okay, we'll talk later I'm sure."

Now that our two Wayshowers know that they have a great responsibility ahead of them. Paul said this, after he sat down next to her "You know Margo this is an excellent opportunity that we have been given."

She then said, very quietly "you are so right, not many people know they are from another galaxy."

Paul chuckled, and said "I don't want to do the math. Remember they said there are only 144,000 of us throughout the world." Paul was a planner and Margo a free spirit.

After traveling for a few hours, it was time for the group's first stop, and a driver change. Margo and Paul were sitting with Greg and Tammy, and some others at the table, when Greg said "well Paul you get to drive next."

Paul looked at Margo and said "yes I do, we all pitch in."

Margo smiled, she wanted to kiss him, but just said "I have some writing to do anyway." Paul thought *and I will be working on our plans, for when we get back home.* She sat alone, pulled her notebook out of her bag, and was ready to put their last dreams into words.

Wisdom

Chemistry is the knowing and revealing,
helping to validate what we are concealing.

This can be complicated in many a way,
so just listen to your thoughts each and every day.

Spirit is energy in an infinite sense,
Moving like a tiger without a fence.

To know what your purpose is to be,
Will liberate your mind and make you free.

When the fire is the hottest to melt,
It's the energy around you to be felt.

Margo Brown 1969

The bus stops in Richmond, Virginia for the night, there Paul grabs Margo's suitcase with his, and asked her "what room are you in?"

"213 thank you" she says smiling at him.

He drops her bags off at the door, and says "let's go for a walk and get a bite to eat in an hour."

She stretches "that will do me a lot of good to stretch my legs and feed my tummy."

Paul smiled at her and said "you have a special way about you."

In the room Tammy said "well you even have him carrying your bags, now that's service."

Margo unpacked for the night and said "I really like this guy."

Three knocks on the door, "Margo, are you ready?" Paul asked while still outside.

Tammy opened the door "she's just finishing up Casanova."

"You're a riot, do you know that?"

Then the bathroom door opens. "I'm ready, let me grab my notebook, and we can go. By the way, where are we going?"

Paul put his finger on his chin and said "I found a diner in the phone book about three blocks away."

On the walk she said "I brought my notebook so you can read my poems."

"That's great, I've been meaning to ask you to do that" he then reached for her hand.

The walk was brisk and the weather was hot so they were ready to sit and enjoy some iced tea. "Hum let's see, mashed potatoes, beans and cornbread. That's what I want and some iced tea" Paul told the waitress.

"How about you dear?" she said to Margo.

"Thanks, I'll have the fish sandwich with the rice, and some iced tea, please."

Paul asked her "can I see your notebook?"

"Sure here it is, I hope you like them."

He looked them over and then after their meal he said "1960, wow you were young then."

"Yes my mom helped me write back then, and she still helps me today." She had a warm feeling after saying that.

Paul then put down the notebook, and said "darling that is beautiful, and we get to see her in our dreams."

"So any favorites?" she said trying not to cry.

He smiled, and said "yes the first one because you write about how beautiful this Earth is." They would talk again, and again about her poems.

They decided to have some hot tea, and pie so Paul asked the waitress "do you have any herbal tea?"

Who then looked at him funny and said "no, I'm sorry sir."

Margo looked in her bag and said "please bring us some hot water then."

Now Paul had a question for her "Margo let's try something in our next dream together."

She looked puzzled and said "okay, what?"

He then explained to her "I have tried to ask my Guide certain questions and when I'm asleep I forget them."

"What do you want to ask?"

"Well if we are together then, let's ask some important questions like; is Jesus real, and where is he, or can we really move mountains, or walk on water?" he said in kind of a young boys inquisitive manner.

"Okay let's do it then."

That night they were taken back to the council, and somehow working together, they did remember to ask one question. "Paul it looks like we are together again in our dream."

Paul looked around and said "yes and we are back at the council. Hello Ringo and Terames."

Margo smiled and said "okay Paul, where are our bodies physically, what city?" she said testing him.

"We are in Richmond, Virginia."

Then she gasped, and said "we want to ask them some questions, right?"

"Yes!" he said.

They looked at one another, trying to remember them, and Margo blurted out to Terames "is Jesus real?"

Terames laughed and said "we are all real in our imaginations."

After some thought about their question, Ambrosia spoke, and said "children, we understand that you have many questions, and although we have the answers to them, we are limited with our time here for questions. With that said, I will attempt to explain who Jesus was, is, and will be to your people of Earth."

The High Councilor went on to explain this. The last thing the two Wayshowers remembered was looking at each other, and thinking of how lucky they are.

CHAPTER 9

Paul remembered what he was told by Amerorth on how powerful our hearts really are, so he jotted down what he had learned.

The heart resonates out energy in the form of a vortex. This vortex of energy has an effect on all that is within it. This is much like the song by The Beach Boys called Good Vibrations. If you use the energy in your heart and combine that with a feeling, good or bad you can have an effect on the situation around you. So we have the power to create, and even control our lives.

Paul Miller 1969

Onward to Alabama they go, with their bags packed, and it's time to load up. It was also a very warm morning in Virginia. Margo was holding her notebook, when Paul said to her "do you want to do some writing?"

She then said, while grabbing his hand, "yes, I want to

preserve the information we were given last night, how about you?"

Paul cleared his throat, and said "I wrote something this morning."

She looked into his eyes, and said "read it to me please."

He grabbed his journal and read what he learned about the heart. She sat back, hugged herself and then wrote.

Live in Love

Jesus said Love is in us all,
Love for blessings big and small.

We can't feel this Love alone from the Heart,
To Love one another other makes us one part.

To be given the keys to life is a good thing to know,
It's an opportunity to accept wisdom and to grow.

I can't by myself do anything with meaning,
All alone the Heart is limited to only dreaming.

Cast out all your fear and worry,
Embrace Love and please, please hurry.

Margo Brown 1969

The stop in Atlanta, Georgia was memorable, and also Paul's grandparents lived in the area. He got off the bus, grabbed their bags, then looked at Margo, and said "let's get into our rooms first, and then I'll call them."

She laughed, and sounding like a woman in love, she said "Let's go!"

His Grandparents are going to pick them up at the hotel,

and take them to dinner. Paul was very happy to have them meet her, and to talk with his grandpa about the latest aircraft he was working on.

After dinner, they returned to the hotel, where Paul asked Margo "let's go for a walk, I see the Peachtree Creek is nearby."

She was so happy after meeting his grandparents, ahe said "yes! Let's go the evening is still young" she had always wanted to say that.

There was a little coffee shop by the creek, and they stopped there briefly. When the coffee was cold, Paul said "let's walk down to the creek." Margo said nothing, she just smiled, reached out her hand, and he took it, then off they went.

This evening they would not be together in their dreams, but they would dream of each other. Their Guides knew that this was part of The Plan for life on this planet, and they weren't needed this night. All he could think about was how much he loved this young woman from eastern Indiana. Before he turned in for the night he said to himself *she is the one for me and I want to marry her*. Paul went to sleep with that thought in mind.

Now she on the other hand, could only think of one thing. Tammy asked her "wow, you are glowing girl, what happened?"

Margo was in too good of a mood to sidestep questions tonight. "Okay, I'll tell you what happened. After dinner with his grandparents we were brought back here. When they left, Paul asked me to go to the creek with him. We talked and had some coffee, then got up, and walked down to the creek." She left out something very important, but not on purpose.

"Margo, there's something else!"

"Oh yes, there is something else. When we were by the water, he took both of my hands, looked me right in the eyes, and said "Margo, I love you" she then sighed.

Tammy was not completely satisfied with that answer "did you kiss him?

She then looked at her friend, and with a big hug of herself, she said "Oh yes, oh yes I kissed him."

Margo had her notebook in hand, she needed to write before turning in. "Tammy dear it's getting late, and I need to write something before I sleep" she said pointing to her notebook.

"Okay girl you write about you, and Casanova. Goodnight dear friend, pleasant dreams."

Our Creation

I have been so happy these days,
my life has been blessed in so many ways.

We are Spirits in these bodies this I know,
and to tune into them our senses will flow.

Remember that life brings on many a pleasure,
good and bad we create them to be our treasure.

Sometimes we lose the ones we love,
knowing they have returned home above.

Love is more than a feeling to show,
love is the power to create what we know.

My life is going to change again soon,
to bloom like the flowers in the month of June.

Margo Brown 1969

Getting two Wayshowers married was never included in the plan, but it did offer some powerful possibilities. Therefore Ambrosia and the rest of the council were very excited.

"Okay, okay quiet" proclaimed Leto.

When Ambrosia stood up she said "we need to take full advantage of these two failing in love."

Both Hermes and Lycus were discussing their plans with Terames and Ringo. "What ideas have you come up with about them?" asked Ambrosia.

Lycus spoke up, and said "Your Grace, we would like to not interfere in their love life. What we propose is to give them the secrets that will help them to be successful in their lives."

Then before Ambrosia could ask another question Hermes spoke. "Your Grace if I may continue with what Lycus said. We also spoke with Margo's mom, and with her insight, we've decided to have specific times when we visit them in their dreams."

Now this will not prevent Margo or Paul from asking to join them when they sleep, they will always have that opportunity. Ambrosia was very pleased with their plan, and said "this will work out to help them achieve our goals. Terames you are to be commended for your work."

"Thank you Your Grace, it is such an honor to receive praise from you."

Dardanus then said "Your Grace, I make a motion that Terames be promoted to Chief." Terames said nothing but she felt so honored that she shed a couple of tears.

Hermes said loudly "I second that motion."

Lycus joined in with "me three!"

Ambrosia closed the session, and said "we now have a new Chief again."

On the last leg of the bus ride back, Paul and Margo were even more inseparable. This only could mean that their lives are going to change soon.

Paul was now even more excited about their trip to Eastern Indiana. They've planned this since coming back from Woodstock. Now it was time to go on the road. "Dear do you have everything that you want to bring? How about those albums you bought for Billy?"

"Stop worrying my Prince, I have it all under control."

Just one planned stop for the night near Louisville, Kentucky and then drive in the next morning. "Fort Knox, that's where they sent my dad after he was drafted, then they shipped him over to Korea to operate on the soldiers." Paul said.

Margo told him "yes, my daddy was over there too."

"Hey maybe they met each other over there."

She laughed "wouldn't that be a hoot."

The car had barely stopped before she started running and yelling "daddy, daddy, I've missed you so much."

Connor was sitting on the porch waiting, then got up, and started running towards her too. "Oh my dear sweet Margo, how have you been?"

"Just fine daddy, where is Billy?"

He then looked over at the house, and said "he just got back from town, so he'll be right out shortly."

She looked back at the car, and said "Ok, I've got a surprise for him."

Billy went over to their car to help Paul unpack, and said "wow a Chevy Fleetline, what year is it?"

"1946, I borrowed it from my dad. Isn't she a beauty?"

Billy looked at the car and said "completely."

They brought the bags inside then Connor reached out his hand, and said "glad to meet you Mr. Miller."

Paul shook his hand, and said "it's just Paul to you sir." Margo stood by with a big smile.

After getting settled in, Paul asked Billy "So Billy, what was it like in Vietnam?"

"Well it was very hot and humid there all the time. When it would stop raining, then the sun would come out, and create a steamer."

Margo interrupted, and said "Billy I brought you some albums of rock bands you like."

He looked them over, and said "Led Zeppelin, Pink Floyd, cool thanks! Hey, I've got an album of a band from Detroit called The Third Power, they're pretty good." Margo took a look, and they listened to them later that evening.

They got settled in for dinner, by being two bachelors, Connor, and Billy became pretty good cooks.

Margo had told Paul that, her family knew about her dreams. Now Paul had met her mom in their dreams, before meeting her dad, and brother.

Connor asked them "how was Woodstock?"

Paul said "it had its moments, but mostly we spent the time getting to know each other."

Connor looked at Margo and smiled.

She went on to tell him "we both had a dream that we were in together."

Connor said "you mean you dreamt of each other?"

"Yes daddy and we had the exact same dream where we communicated with each other. We later learned that we are both Wayshowers from the Pleiades."

He really didn't know what to say except "that is amazing, sounds like the two of you are old souls."

Paul said "I couldn't believe it, I met Elizabeth there. Her name is Terames, and she sits on the High Council of the Pleiades."

They turned in for the night but, before that, Connor, and Billy read her poems. "Dear these are great! This reminds me of when your mom would help you write." he said, while missing her.

"Thank you daddy, she still helps me in my dreams" she said, and then gave him a big hug.

Connor then said "well kids I guess it's time to turn in for the night."

I believe that night Terames wanted to be with all of her Earthly family. Even though Margo and Paul were in separate rooms they still were together in their dreams.

"Ambrosia, Your Grace, it is an honor to be in your company again" said Paul bowing at the waist.

Ambrosia looked at him, and said with a smile "you sir are a gentleman, we are so glad you, and the lovely Margo are back." Margo just did the best curtsy she could.

Tonight was going to be a very special night. Once everyone was settled in, Leto made the Announcement "for working so hard to help planet Earth achieve her mission, we proudly promote elder Terames, from the star Maia to Chief elder."

She was then called up to report to Ambrosia, to then receive her citation, and new uniform. Margo was so proud of her mom that she couldn't wait to congratulate her. She, and Paul walked over, then she hugged her, and said "mom you are an inspiration to me that transcends Earth."

He bowed to her and said "Chief Terames."

"Now to business," Ambrosia said, paused then said "Margo, your mom has asked to still be your Guide. Since she would be your mentor, then the only way for this to work would be for her to teach you how to be a Chief."

"Your Grace, I will work hard and learn all I can from her."

"That's good to hear, now Mr. Miller she will need all of your support."

He stood up and said "she will get it all Your Grace."

After a long break, they returned with some instructions from the plan. Ambrosia spoke to them "Paul you and Margo are to be given some secrets tonight. Hermes or Lycus please elaborate."

They both looked at each other then shook their heads in the affirmative, and Lycus said "Chief Terames, if you would please."

Terames stood up, and waived for the two of them to come over to her. She then said to them "Although these secrets are very simple, our people on Earth can't seem to understand how they work. Here it is; whatever you focus your attention on that is what you will receive, good or bad."

They both looked at each other, and then Margo asked her "do you mean that if we want something all we have to do is focus our attention on it, and it will happen?"

They woke up the next morning, and couldn't wait to see each other. She finished in the bathroom, hurried downstairs, just to find all three sitting at the table drinking coffee. With a big smile Paul said to her "good morning dear, did you sleep well last night?"

"Paul you know how well I slept, we both went to the council last night, and saw mom get her promotion."

Putting his coffee cup down, Connor said "promotion, promotion to what?"

Paul smiled at Margo, and then answered him "to Chief elder of Maia."

She then raised her hands up and said "I love my mom."

Before they left to go back to Montgomery, Paul did ask Connor for Margo's hand in marriage, and said he was going to ask her the question the week after they returned.

He asked for her hand at the same restaurant, that his dad took mom too, and proposed. Their wedding was just as spectacular, only this time it was junior, and his girl from Indiana. Cobbs Lake wasn't as uninhabited as it was twenty some years ago. Paul even cut his hair for the occasion and Margret was oh so beautiful. She wore the traditional white gown, the top fell just below her collarbone, and the design was simple yet gorgeous.

They decided to travel to the Denver, Colorado area for their honeymoon. Summer was coming and Paul thought it would be a great place for Margo to do some writing. Breathing in the mountain and the day after going up Pikes Peak, Margo was so inspired.

Years go by and these two are so in love. Knowing the day will come when their baby arrives, Margo decides to write, and pour out her feelings of these wonderful years.

Life is a Vapor

Years go by and I am so thrilled,
this life is my garden to be tilled.

I plant seeds which I create in Love,
then I nourish them with care of.

Since time goes by in a flash,
why would I need a stash?

To give what I have to those in need,
I will then realise the mustard seed.

The Master's teachings are a light to this Earth,
they are given to our Spirits for a new berth.

I can communicate with all the life around,
vibrations of Love to all that abound.

Animals are creations just like me,
I learn to love all that I see.

Margo Brown Miller 1972

Little baby Tamla that is her name. Margo wanted to name her Terames after her mom, but Paul talked her out of it. She was born three months ago, and the Miller's planning to have a big family get together soon.

Connor and Billy haven't seen the new member yet, and are travelling down to Montgomery, to see her, and to visit the rest.

It's a beautiful Saturday on the farm when Connor and Billy arrive. Later that evening Paul Sr. asks Billy about Vietnam "so son you've been across the world in the military too."

"Yes sir thirteen months in country making airstrips."

Connor then said to Paul Sr. "I convinced him to join the Air Force before they drafted him."

Paul Sr. agreed with that, and said "I had Paul in college under the same deferment that I took advantage of during WWII."

Connor and Paul Sr. both chuckled about that.

Connor nodding yes, said "good move, but I heard they did draft you for Korea."

"Yes they did what a nasty war."

"Tell me about it, I was in the 7th Infantry Division during the Frozen Chosin. Who were you with?"

Paul Sr. looked at him curiously, and said "a couple of M.A.S.H. units."

"I had to go to them a few times and pick up my men after they were healed."

A chill went right down Paul Sr.'s spine, and he said "you're Sgt. Brown aren't you?"

"Yes I was a Sargent, why?"

"I'm Capt. Miller and you came one time when I was on duty and picked up your men." This was a big deal for these two men, they both thought how small this planet really is. ("Wouldn't that be a hoot" Margo Brown 1969.)

Margo and Lucille were both enjoying time together, while grandma was holding little Tamla. They lived on a little farm where Margo just loved the animals so much, just like when she was a little girl back home in Indiana. Paul's parents went back home, Paul and Margo talked with Connor, and Billy about meeting Dorothy the next day.

Warriors

These men do not want to kill or to maim,
to want to do that would be insane.

Knowing firsthand that war is hell,
that is what they wish to tell.

To go through such anguish is very hard,
and the Heart will be forever scarred.

Honor them for just being brave,
the real heroes are in the grave.

When they come together to relate,
it will heal their wounds to resonant.

So just Love them for who they are,
not remember a time or a place very far.

Margo Brown Miller 1972

She hadn't seen their baby yet, so this was a surprise. The store door opens, they enter then Dorothy leaves the counter, and says with her arms open "let me hold that sweet little girl."

Margo knew that Dorothy would just adore her. "What's her name?" asked Dorothy.

"Her name is Tamla, I wanted to name her after my mom,

but since mom's name is now Terames, we picked this one because it felt close to it."

She looked at Tamla and said "it suits her fine."

Paul then told Dorothy "she is in our dreams, and Terames said she is an Indigo child."

Dorothy looked at them and said "she is very special indeed." After all that commotion, Dorothy noticed the two men standing next to them, and said "hello?"

Margo then spoke, and said "Dorothy this is my dad, Connor Brown, and my brother Billy."

"So you came all the way down from Indiana?"

Connor said "yes, and it's a privilege to meet you. You've helped these two through a lot of difficult times."

CHAPTER 10

144,000 Wayshowers are coming of age. Let's meet several of them that live in the area of the Millers, for these Wayshowers will be instrumental in helping Margo and Paul achieve their purpose.

She was born in the city of Atlanta, Georgia, her parents both worked in the textile mills, and her name is Jennifer Knowles. She was twenty-one when she asked the Great Spirit to help her, her visitor is from the star Alcyone, and they met one night in 1972.

Before turning in for the night, she said this in her prayers "Lord please, send one of your Angels down to visit me in my dreams. I need some help, with my current situation." She was in her last year of college, and found out she was pregnant. That night in her dreams, she was surprised, and said "who are you?"

This strange looking visitor replied "well, you might want

to call me an Angel, but I'm really just someone from your star called Alcyone."

She was almost speechless, but did ask "What?"

This visitor went on to explain "okay you asked to have a visit from an Angel tonight to help you. Well, I'm no Angel, but I will be your Guide from now on. And don't worry I will send people to help you with your baby." She then woke up for school, and felt like she had just returned from a two week vacation in Maui.

His name is Cory Greene and he lives just outside of Mobile, Alabama. In school he was always bored, except in his math classes. He would sit in them, and think about working on his hot rod after school. "Mr. Greene, what are you doing?" asked Mrs. Flanks, who was his English composition 102 teacher.

He closed his notepad, put his pencil down and said "just listening to your lecture Mrs. Flanks."

She then turned around, and said "we'll see how much you've listened. Class study chapter 7, and write a 5000 word easy due next week."

Cory was set on getting his degree in mechanical engineering, and then hopefully going to Detroit, Michigan, and design sports cars. He was also interested in UFO's, especially how they would fly so fast, but his first love was fast cars.

It was 1973 when he was in his second year of college, and after serving two years in the Marine Corp. He would sometimes think about his time in the Corp, and all the young men he knew that would do drugs, or drink a lot of alcohol. The questions he would ask himself were "God, why do people get so depressed, and try to destroy their selves?" This bothered him so much that one night before going to sleep he prayed "please Jesus, give me the answers as to why this happens, and protect me from this."

That evening he would be visited from the star of Merope. His visitor startled him in his sleep, and said "Cory, are you dreaming about sports cars?"

He replied in his sleep, while knowing it was a dream, "of course, who and what are you?"

"I'm from Merope one of seven stars in the Pleiades cluster."

He then woke up, and said "what was that all about?" It was 1:11 in the morning and he then went back to sleep.

Spending the first seventeen years of your life in a Parochial school, might cause you to want a change. Katherine Allison was born in 1962, in a little Parish outside of New Orleans, Louisiana. She was planning on going to college in South Bend, Indiana at Notre Dame, and her parents were very happy with her until.

"Mom, Dad, I'm not sure if I'm ready to go to college right now." Even though they were understanding parents, her not going to college, was just impossible for them to even contemplate.

Mom grabbed her hands, and said "dear, what do you want to do?" Dad was standing there holding his breath.

She then said "Some of my friends are going to Pensacola, Florida, to hang out for a few days on the beach. I want to go with them, and clear my head before I think about college."

Dad then said "without question the answer is no."

The beach is so nice, and some friends brought some weed, and wine to share. She had never touched either, and at first said "no" when asked to partake.

As the evening wore on, one of the boys said "I guess you

still think you're back in Catholic school."

That made her mad, and she said "give me that." Several hours later, and three sheets to the wind, she was just the way they wanted her.

Waking up hurt, and feeling used, she was ready to go home. The call came "can you come and pick me up?" she said crying.

Her dad answered, and instead of being angry, he said "yes, my little girl, where are you?" She told him, and he said "my Angel, we are on our way." They brought her back home.

That night before bed, Katherine would pray "Mary, mother full of grace, please help me to understand what just happened. Send your Angels to comfort me, and guide me in my life." Feeling safe in her room, she fell asleep. "Who are you? You don't look like an Angel?"

"I am from the star called Sterope which is one of the seven stars of the Pleiades."

"Why are you in my dream?"

"I am your Guide, to help you learn of where you are from, and that you are a Wayshower from my star" She woke the next morning with a determination to go to school, and to please her parents.

That summer was hot, hot and very humid in Jackson, Mississippi. It seemed like as soon as one storm would leave, another was right behind it. Poor Joey was working on dad's roofing business, and with all the storms they couldn't do their jobs. At twenty years old, he was home from college, and trying to make some money for his junior year. Dad told him "don't worry son, we'll get plenty of work in as soon as these storms clear."

Now there doesn't have to be an event, to wake up a

Wayshower, and this was the case. Joey had become interested in the meta-physical world, and bought a couple of books at a store near his campus. While shut-in, he said to his parents "well with all this rain, I'm going to my room to read."

Dad said "okay son, enjoy." This book he was reading, was about calling to the Masters, and asking to be taught in the ways of enlightenment.

By the time evening had come around, Joey had read for a few hours. With school, and work he hadn't been able to dedicate this much time for this type of reading. After eating some of mom's home cooking, he went back up to his room and read until he fell asleep. There he would read about the Atlantis civilization, how it was destroyed, about the Masters, and their teachings. The one area he was intrigued with was dreams, and how to contact the Masters, and ask to be taken spiritually somewhere in them.

Asleep finally, he said "Master who are you?"

The strange looking visitor said "well Joey Morgan I'm no Master, not even a Chief, but I am here to be your Guide."

He then looking at his visitor said "okay, what are you going to teach me?"

"Slow down, you need to know who you are, and where you are from first. You, and I, are from the same star called Taygete, and you are a Wayshower."

He then thought for a minute and asked "what's a Wayshower?"

"Country music, that's what ya'll find here" she said. That's just how Rebecca (Becky) Tennant feels about her hometown of Nashville, Tennessee. She doesn't hate country music, but she's always found that most of it to be so depressing and it's also what her parents like. Now rock and roll music is a whole different thing, and the type she does like is called progressive rock. You can read books about the meta-physical world or you can find a lot of information in progressive rock music.

She is twenty six years old, a class of 1983 graduate from the University of Tennessee with an MBA. She is a professional woman. Streets are moving along normal, this Tuesday morning, and she's late for a meeting with some executive's from Japan. Very high strung and goal oriented she wants desperately to move up the ladder. As her anger of being late sets in, she says out loud "why can't I get to work on time? I left 30 minutes early this morning!" At the end of the day it all worked out, and on her drive home she said "why was I so nervous and jumpy this morning? The meeting went well and now it's all behind me."

That same evening she was meeting an old friend for dinner. One she looked forward to seeing again. She wanted everything to be perfect for her friend. Becky was early and while waited for her friend she thought, *let's see I leave for work early, and still get there late. I leave a little late for dinner and I'm early. There has to be a logical reason for all this.*

They hadn't seen each other in a couple of years. Then her friend Judy arrives, and says "Becky, how have you been? Two years is too long to be without my best friend."

She stands up, then gives her a big hug, and says "Oh Judy, how I've missed your calm demeanor now let's talk." As they are talking Becky notices that the things her friend is saying seems to strike right at the heart of her problems. "What do you mean by, I create my own reality?"

Judy replies very calmly "dear friend we control our lives by the thoughts and feelings we create."

She then tilted her head to the right and said "is it that

simple?"

Judy smiled and said "not really, we need to be conscious of our thoughts, because when we attach feelings to them they will become our reality."

Becky being a very well read, eager to learn person, wanted more of this information quickly. She then asked before they left "what can I do to control my thoughts?"   "Tonight before going to sleep, ask Jesus to send a visitor to you in your dreams. Tell him you want answers to why you are a Wayshower." They were leaving and she didn't get a chance to ask Judy what a Wayshower is.

On her drive home from dinner she had a cassette tape of Queens's album named A Night at the Opera in her tape player with their big hit Bohemian Rhapsody playing, which she loved. This album was released by Elektra Records in the United States. The words from that song were so apropos for her dream that night. "Is this the real life? Or is this just fantasy...?"

Returning to her apartment she felt the need to sit and relax with a cup of herbal tea. She sat there calmly reflecting on her conversation with Judy. *She seemed so calm and in control of things. I wish I could be more like her. This stress is really getting to be too much. I'll ask Jesus for help tonight.* Little did she know that, at that moment she was already doing exactly what her friend talked about.

Becky was about to find out some answers in her dream that night. Seeing an elven type person, she asked "Who are you?"

"Hello Becky, I'm from the Pleiadian star Electra."

Then Becky tilted her head from side to side, said "okay, why do you look different?"

"You look the same when you're not in that body. We are from the same star and you are here as a Wayshower."

Her body went cold and she thought *that's what Judy said about me being a Wayshower.*

The Harmonic Convergence is to be held on August 15-17, 1987 at Mount Shasta, California. There will be other places throughout the world for all of the 144,000 Wayshowers to gather for this event. With all of the Wayshowers now awake and aware of who they are the High Council has a short time to get them all together.

CHAPTER 11

Councilor Ambrosia was excited because of this urgency. Leto started the meeting with "your Grace, we have a few Earth months to assemble the Wayshowers, for the alignment of the planets in their solar system."

Aethusa stood up and confirmed "yes, we have been studying some of the ways to accomplish this."

Sinon said "yes so far we've used books to get them prepared for this day."

Ambrosia replied "you all have done a great job so far, but there are some that have just come to the knowledge of their own divinity. Does anyone know of any other means there are to use?" And then a former human asked to speak. "Yes, you have something to say Terames."

She then answered "your Grace, we can use radio and television to get the message out."

"That is a good idea, let's address that later."

Then one night all the Wayshowers were given the same message.

Tamla was turning fifteen and she had a heart of gold. Her mom would read stories to her about the Pleiades and how they will return there one day. She was schooled by her mom because she was advised by the High Council to do so. They agreed to home school her because they understood that the school system would try and change her too much.

This evening the Millers were to receive instructions from Terames and Ringo. After sixteen plus years of visiting the Millers they were very comfortable in their dreams. Tamla started the dream with "grandma, how are you?"

"I am fine darling. I have something important to tell all of you tonight." Once they were all attentive to her she said "in August of this year you need to make a trip to Mt. Shasta, California. This will be a gathering of Wayshowers in North America."

After a day of helping the children at her school Katherine was so tired. *Now to take my shoes off, and fix dinner* was her thought. Katherine (Kathy) loved to cook and her husband enjoyed it too. He wasn't due home for another thirty minutes so a little wine while she mixed the sauce will be fine. Bob was a good religious man, but didn't know about Kathy being a Wayshower.

That evening she made them some tea and he asked her "how was your day, dear?"

Kathy pouring tea said "just the normal chaos with the children. How about you, was your work pleasant?"

Bob answered her with a thought he had instead "we need

to travel somewhere. I think a change would be good for us." He couldn't have been more right.

It's a funny thing to have as Edgar Poe said *a dream within a dream*, but to wake up inside a dream is different. Kathy was sound asleep when her visitor said "Kathy, wake up."

She, then feeling very strange said "how can I "wake up" if you're part of my dream?"

Her visitor answered with "leave your other dream, I have something to tell you."

Her reply was simply "okay, space alien from the star Electra that visits me in my dreams, and tells me that I am a Wayshower from the same star as they are. How can I help you?"

Her new friend said "that's nice, now down to business. You will need to travel to Mt. Shasta, California in August of this year." She then woke up and went to work.

Joey Morgan, Rebecca Tennant, Cory Greene, and Jennifer Knowles all got the same message from their guides. Now the question was how to get them there? I'm sure some Wayshowers with many more years of experience will have a plan.

Mother Earth

Alive, the Earth wants us to come,
with a knowledge that's greater in some.

Together we make her come alive,
in this we never need to strive.

Light will not hide from winter to fall,
and her people are ready to answer the call.

Our shadows are very tall,
created by the Light, that's in us all.

When we come to meditate,
Mother Earth will celebrate.

Blessed so that day will be,
we give our hearts to her you see.

Margo Brown Miller 1987

He had been a family doctor for many years and in his spare time (outside of golf and tennis) he would read and study about the Quantum Theory. What this did for Dr. Paul Miller Jr. MD was to help him understand that we are Spirits inhabiting these physical bodies. All the while this knowledge always left him thinking there must be more for our Spirits to inhabit because these bodies do die.

When you read what all the Masters said, especially in the Bible, you need to compare what they said by what they've said before. The Master Jesus said to John in the book of John 14:2 "In my Father's house are many mansions: if it were not so, I would have told you. I go to prepare a place for you."

Now you might think a home, like the ones with doors and windows, but when you read what the Master Paul describes it would mean something different. To read in I Corinthians 15:50 "Now this I say, brethren that flesh and blood cannot inherit the kingdom of God..."

Paul Miller always believed the words written on this subject meant that we would receive a new body and probably

Jesus was wearing the new one when he was down here. Margo would listen to him explain this and this is what she made of it.

Spirits Inhabit

To walk on water is not the norm,
although Jesus did, while in his form.

If we question the reasons why,
our faith will weaken, and not even try.

There are many miracles put in our way,
so open your heart, and seize the day.

When we open up ourselves to know,
our Spirits are ready to join the show.

The Sun will rise and set each day,
and the moon is in Love in a special way.

That we are part of all that is found,
even the forms that make no sound.

I end with this one thought,
awake, your desires are sought.

Margo Brown Miller 1987

This current dream will expand hundreds of Earth miles and use a lot of energy. Back at the High Council the Chiefs were discussing their plan.

"Where are the Guides supposed to take them to?" asked Aethusa.

Leto was prepared for that question and said "they will be taken to the base on the moon to receive instructions."

Ambrosia said "our Wayshowers are ready to be brought together in groups to prepare for the convergence."

The chiefs were then given instructions from Leto "you will need to coordinate with their Guides to choose one from each group to lead."

Dr. Miller was talking with his family about their trip to Mt. Shasta, California in a couple of months. There is a lot of truth to that old saying "let the Spirit move you." Tonight the Miller family where moving in their Spirits and after dinner Paul said "girls let's have some tea and meditate before we visit Terames and Ringo tonight."

Both Margo and Tamla were in agreement, they felt something special about the evening. Their "tea time" before meditation was intended for them to talk about what is on their minds and to help clear it for meditation.

Later that evening when the moon was bright their Guides arrived. Paul was the first to speak "hello Ringo and Terames how are things back in the Pleiades?" their relationship had grown to where they all were family.

Nothing seemed different until Terames said "follow me." She had them follow her and Ringo into a meeting room.

Margo said after entering the room "what is this meeting for?"

Terames then said "sit down please and observe the screen." As they were watching the screen a plan was being shown. Terames was seated next to her granddaughter Tamla and was very happy.

Paul looked at them, smiled and said "we are to lead a group from the area to the convergence." After he said that, Dorothy from the bookstore entered the room and sat next to Margo.

Just minutes passed when the doors opened and a group of five people entered. The Millers stood up to greet them and Ringo said "these are your fellow Wayshowers representing each star and from your Earth area. Wayshowers these are the Millers, Paul, Margo, and Tamla. They are from Montgomery, Alabama and they will be the leaders of this group."

Terames then introduced the five Wayshowers; Jennifer Knowles from Atlanta, Georgia, Joey Morgan from Jackson, Mississippi, Cory Greene from Mobile, Alabama, Katherine Allison from New Orleans, Louisiana, and Rebecca Tennant from Nashville, Tennessee

Then Margo took charge and said "okay, now to business. We have a short time to co-ordinate this. We will need to get all of your contact information, and since this is a dream, that information might not transfer into our 3D world, so here's what we will do. We will meet at Dorothy's meta-physical bookstore seven days from now. She is located in Montgomery near the campus."

CHAPTER 12

It was 18 years ago, practically to the day that both Paul and, Margo were on the trip that changed their lives. I suppose this trip was a large step in (giving back). He met her at Woodstock then, and now they are going to Mt. Shasta with their fifteen year old Indigo daughter named Tamla.

Loves Purpose

Time moves in many ways,
just basking in the sun's rays.

This life is a beautiful ride,
follow your pure Love from inside.

Love will create Love for all,
for it's given to us from the call.

Don't hide your Love this time,
you should let it show, and shine.

Margo Brown Miller 1987

A week has passed since their dreams together. The Wayshowers where to all met at Dorothy's store today. The Miller's had arrived early, so they could be prepared to greet the others as they arrived. After some time of visiting with Dorothy, Cory Greene arrived.

Paul went up to his car to greet him "hello Cory how was the drive?"

He answered and said "fine sir, you must be Dr. Paul Miller."

"Yes I am, come on inside and we'll wait for the others." The rest arrived there by noon which was the agreed upon time.

They spent that afternoon realizing how they were all in the same dream, and how it brought them to travel there. Tamla was tasked to get their contact information and Margo organized the logistics of the trip. She said to Paul "we are going to follow a lot of what we did when your medical group travelled to Woodstock in 1969."

"That's a great idea. If anyone needs any help financially or otherwise to be able to go just give me a call."

Then they all finished their business and headed home.

The High Council met several times before the Wayshowers left on their trip to Mt. Shasta. On one such occasion Ambrosia said to Terames "your daughter Margo is really becoming a leader on Earth. I guess she gets that from you."

"Thank you Your Grace you say the most wonderful and inspiring things."

"I am well pleased with her and she is training your granddaughter Tamla the same way."

Ringo and Terames were having a conversation about the trip. When Leto approached them and said "tell the Millers that there are Avatars in place to help provide them with what they need for the trip to Mt. Shasta." They both shook their heads in the affirmative.

Ringo said to Terames "let's separate them in their dreams so we can concentrate on giving them the information they will need."

"Good idea, I'll visit the girls and you handle Paul. Don't forget we will need to update the other Guides on what we are doing."

A bus was provided from someone Paul knew at work. On one day he mentioned to one of his nurses "We are getting ready for our family vacation, the one thing we need is a bus for our large family." He didn't know this at the time, but she was the person to tell this too.

"Dr. Miller my uncle has three buses, I'm sure you can borrow one of them."

He was stunned "you're kidding he has three buses, we would gladly rent one of them." They got the bus for a song.

That same night the Miller family dreamed and since the three were so busy trying to plan for this trip, their guides decided to give them a vacation tonight.

Tamla said "daddy this place is amazing."

He looked around and said "yes it is. Where are Ringo and Terames?"

Margo looked around too and concluded "they are not here."

Little Tamla said "who cares, I'm going swimming with those two dolphins. They asked me to join them."

They both looked at each other, then Tamla, and Paul said "darling our little girl is enjoying herself let's join in."

The night was spent in the most beautiful bluest green water you could imagine. They would swim, dive, pet, hug and talk to all their aquatic friends.

The next morning the Millers' were so excited and refreshed from the night before. Tamla hugged them both in the kitchen and didn't want to let go, she was just that happy.

She did have one request though and she asked them "when can we go back again?"

"Dear we don't know, but we want to go back too." They went out and did their chores and prepared for their trip.

Margo thought about the vacation dream she and her immediate family had so she needed to write something to honor their friends in the dream.

Aquatic Hearts

Our beautiful friends of the water,
who live their lives with no border.

They have a special way,
filling our hearts with Love all day.

Their hearts give out Love to be show,
for when we feel sad, and are all alone.

We long for them to be our companions,
these water friends your Love fills this canyon.

Margo Brown Miller 1987

The Harmonic Convergence is the name given to one of the world's first globally synchronized meditation events, which occurred on August 16–17, 1987, which also closely coincided with an exceptional alignment of planets in our solar system. An important part of the Harmonic Convergence observances was the idea of congregating at "power centers." Power centers were places, such as Mount Shasta, California, and Mount Fuji, where the spiritual energy was held to be particularly strong. The belief was that if 144,000 people assembled at these power centers and meditated for peace, that the arrival of the new era would be facilitated. WikipediA

Time to get on the bus, for this day has arrived, and it will take them a few days to get there. They would all become like a family along the way. The drive was long but the scenery on the way was magnificent. Travelling through the Ozarks, the Rockies, the Painted desert, and then up the coastline of California.

The group would talk about their Guides and the star that they are from. Now this was not your typical group of tourists; these people were knowledgeable of some pretty amazing things. Someone even had a copy of Tony Shearer's book *Lord of the Dawn* and that helped enlighten them. Some of the Wayshowers brought their families along and they were quickly enlightened.

Upon arrival Margo got the group together and said "since we are from the south, let's call ourselves the Rebels. This way we can just say rebels let's get our tents put up and make camp before dark." With that said, the rebels responded and put up the camp together quickly.

Paul just smiled and said to Tamla "your mom sure is a leader."

The next day began with breakfast, both Paul and Margo reminisced from their time at Woodstock. Later that day was spent in classes on how they would harmonize that evening. They had about two hours before the harmonic convergence was to start.

So Paul asked Margo and Tamla "girls help me round up the rebels for dinner and for fellowship time." They all went out to find them.

Sitting around the fire Paul would tell stories of how he and Margo met at Woodstock. Kathy asked him "when did you fall in love with her."

"Beside the Peachtree creek in Atlanta on our way home from Woodstock." Margo sat there just remembering what a wonderful night that was.

They were getting up to go and Bob said "you two are so lucky to both be Wayshowers."

Margo looked at Bob and Kathy and said "you two are very lucky to share this time together. Bob even though you don't have the dreams you do believe in your wife and who she is. Remember the Master Jesus said, blessed are those who haven't seen and believe." Even though he wasn't a Wayshower like them, Bob participated just as though he was.

The evening was beautiful up on the mountain and the air really brought your senses to their full capacity. Each group on the mountain was complete with one Wayshower from each star. They noticed the stars and with one voice made a giant harmonic sound. This was done to give their energy to help heal the Earth and set the inhabitants on a path of love. When it was all done for the night the rebels went back to camp and dreamed.

Paul had a dream of the DNA that he had been reading about and Amerorth gave him plenty of information on the moon base that night. When Paul woke up the next morning he wrote in his journal.

I was taken up into the heavens and shown some things that aren't hard to explain but are hard to prove. The day will come when our technology will allow us to prove these ideas. The one I was given was that our DNA has 12 strands and can be plugged back into our 12 Crown Chakra system. I'm not completely sure what this all means but I do intend on researching it.   Dr. Paul Miller MD 1987

After reading this Margo was moved to write something to explain it in a poem form. She was very happy to read Paul's writing about his dreams on the moon base.

Our Substance

Life exists in the tiniest of things,
a mighty power to the life it brings.

We are taken a distance that is far,
to clear the mind and see who we are.

Greater than the sum of all parts,
together shows each one's smarts.

These bands program us into a being,
with our Spirit to love all that it's seeing.

I close with this mystery,
live life and create history.

Margo Brown Miller 1987

CHAPTER 13

The rebels are up eating breakfast, while sitting around talking they formed into little groups, and they had the whole day to enjoy each other's company. In the evening when the stars were out they would join their group and meditate.

As they were talking, Margo said "this is a wonderful thing to come together and meditate for peace on Earth."

Jenny then said to Margo "tell me about it, my daddy was a Marine in the Korean war. I wish there was peace then, and he didn't have to go and fight, it really messed him up."

As she was talking Cory thought about being drafted and said to her "I really feel for the men and women like your dad. I too was drafted but fortunately I didn't have to go to Vietnam."

After breakfast Jenny and Cory kept talking to each other. One of the things he said to her was "what, do you like to do, for fun?"

She just smiled and said "you've met my daughter Shasha,

so right now seeing her grow into a young woman makes me happy."

He liked her answer and told her "I've never been married, seems like I've spent so many years in school and working on cars, that I never made the time to meet the right person."

"Me either, maybe there is a reason for that?" Therefore as the day progressed, these two grew closer and closer.

Sitting down by a tree, Margo was reading a book entitled "Out on a Limb" by Shirley MacLaine. This book really helped her understand a lot of things in the meta-physical world.

Paul walked up and said "what are you reading?"

Looking up at him she said "a book by Shirley MacLaine."

"One of my nurses is a big fan of hers."

She couldn't help but say "really, who?"

He then kissed her and said "I'll introduce you to her when we get back home."

The sun was setting and dinner needed to be made, so all the rebels moved into their camp and started cooking. The way they worked together as a small community was something to behold. There were a few children present, like Tamla and Shasha, and they became good friends. There were no set duties everyone just pitched in and Paul enjoyed cooking so he was behind the skillet.

"What a gorgeous night" exclaimed Becky she said this as she was listening to Led Zeppelin's "Stairway to Heaven" on her Walkman.

Cory and Jenny looked over and could hear her sing. "When one is all and all is one." That's when Cory gently grabbed Jenny's hand. They went from there to the group and began to meditate. There they repeated this mantra "bring peace to our planet and heal all wounds."

Dreams were to be full of light energy that night and this group will have one to remember.

Their Guides met them all, with this greeting "come and enjoy what your future will be like."

There they were on a planet, very much like a new Earth. Jenny looked around to see not only her fellow Wayshowers but their guests too, and she noticed Shasha was next to her.

Shasha said "mommy is this real?"

Not knowing how to answer that, she said "dear it's as real as our imaginations are."

This planet was a future Earth and it was as pristine as can be. The Miller's had been there before so they helped the others enjoy thier visit.

Cory located Jenny and Shasha and said "I would be honored if you girls would experience this with me."

They both took his hand and flew off, up into the clouds. All sorrow, worry, sadness and fear were done away with that night. The water creatures seemed to radiate from the energy that the humans were emanating out. The next morning these rebels were a changed people.

On the bus ride home, the talk for the next three days was so positive and full of love that these Wayshowers were ready to change this world. Jenny and Cory sat together and became very close. Shasha and Tamla talked about the dolphins and compared some of the names they gave them. Paul and Margo both reflected on the trip and thought how great these next twenty-five years will be. Margo wrote this to remember.

Join the Light

Cycles of time are here,
to break the bonds of fear.

In doing this we learned,
all beauty is to be discerned.

Light and Love abound in us all,
hope, peace, and joy we stand tall.

To join all as one we may,
find our courage to follow the Way.

Become one in the light,
then illuminate the night.

Margo Brown Miller 1987

It was family night for the Miller's where this meant it was their weekly meeting with Terames and Ringo. Except for this night they would have them separated for a while.

These dreams start with Tamla running to her grandma and giving her a big hug and then asking her "can we go back and see the dolphins?"

The wonder of this is that Terames didn't miss a thing, by not residing in a physical body on Earth. She was there, although not visible at Margo's wedding, and on the day Tamla was born. But they were given eyes to see the other dimensions of this universe and to see her.

Ringo addressed the family first and said "girls Paul will not be in your dreams for the next few months. He will be spending his time on the moon base with Amerorth."

Paul was excited, but sad at the same time, and said "I had hoped I would be seeing my friend Amerorth again. When I'm done we will go on another family vacation."

The one thing they were learning was to not ask for something in a question. It was more likely to happen if you just stated your desires as something that was going to happen.

The moon base was Paul's favorite place it was his personal galactic laboratory.

Amerorth greeted him "good to see you old friend."

`Paul laughed and said "I hope that's ole friend and not old friend. But then again maybe you're speaking of times past. No matter, it's good to see you too. I'm ready to learn more knowledge of the universe."

"I'm going to teach you about how to live the next twenty-five years."

"What do you mean?"

"There are laws in the universe that can't be broken. I will teach you that by following them you will become one with the Source."

Paul breathed deep and said "that sounds like something I've wanted for years."

Here are a few of the laws Amerorth gave him: what you think about then becomes your reality; how you treat other people will change them; giving is a major function of receiving; If your life is full then there's no room for receiving; direct your good thoughts towards feeling it; breathe in good and breathe out negativity; all things are made from the same energy; never think too highly of yourself; don't judge others but help them if possible; and meditate daily find quiet time to renew.

Paul took all this in and Amerorth said "these sound simple and they are, but they aren't easily followed. We will practice them over the next few months."

He then replied "Amerorth, I can feel how important these laws are to learn and then teach to others."

"I can see you are already on your way to using them daily."

Breakfast for this family is like most others except for one day a week, which is Saturday the day after, they talk about their dreams of being together the before.

This time Paul was getting the eggs ready to scramble when Tamla said "daddy how was your time with Ringo?"

Margo answered her "dear, he might not be able to share that with us yet."

Paul then brought the eggs to the table and said "girls, I'm trying to get my thoughts together and share with you. Let's eat first and then talk."

"Okay daddy."

"Let's have tea and talk" was Margo's response to breakfast being over.

Paul said "you girls tell me about your dream. You were together and I missed being with you."

Margo said "Tamla you start telling your dad about our dream first."

"Okay mom, we spent the evening with grandma, and she took us to the High Council. There we learned about government and the things that are being learned from our time on Earth."

He then said "it doesn't sound as exciting as the dolphins."

She laughed and said "I know daddy but grandma is a leader and she takes care of so much stuff. Mom and I both thought that how great it is to be a leader, and be able to help each other." Margo didn't need to say a word Tamla did just fine.

Now it was his turn and Margo let him know that "okay Paul, dear what did you and Ringo talk about?"

He took a deep breath and said "first Ringo took me to the moon base and then left me with my friend Amerorth. Amerorth spent the time teaching me about DNA and other secrets. I have a few months to learn how to live them and then teach others."

Tamla said "what are the secrets?"

"It isn't complicated or a mystery. It is based on the laws of the universe that don't change, and always work when followed. Some of them are about what you put your attention on becomes your reality, giving is very important in order to receive, and how your actions control situations. Those are just a few we have to train on, in order to follow our heart and not our mind."

"Wow daddy, those are goods things to learn."

Several months after the trip to Mt. Shasta, wedding invitations went out to the rebels.

You are cordially invited.
To attend the wedding of;
Cory Greene
And
Jennifer Knowles
April 20th, 1988
At the home of
Dr. Paul and Margaret Miller
Montgomery, Alabama

CHAPTER 14

"The Berlin Wall was a barrier that divided Berlin from 1961 to 1989, constructed by the German Democratic Republic starting on 13 August 1961 that completely cut off West Berlin from surrounding East Germany and from East Berlin until it was opened in November 1989." WikipediA

Those were some very important years for the Wayshowers and their fellow Boomers. In those twenty-eight years the Avant-garde went from 15 to being 43 years old. That's almost finishing high school to having your children in college.

Speaking of college, Tamla was one year away from going and this brought memories for Margo of what happened to her mother when she was ready to go to college. She felt so honored and grateful to have followed in her mother Elizabeth's footsteps raising such a special kind person. Margo asked Tamla "are you looking to go to college next year?" Knowing that her being homeschooled would be different for.

Tamla said "mom, I'll tell you what I've decided, maybe we can talk later." Margo kissed her goodnight.

Loves Gratitude

Can you see the future ahead?
Does it mean all that is said?

Moments bring you back in time,
maybe it's an old song's catchy rhyme.

Either way we do get there,
for energy travels through the air.

Give out Love in every way,
be a blessing in all they say.

Release negativity out and not exclude,
breathe in the good air with gratitude.

Prepare for magic's spell to carry,
a whimsical Heart that's so merry.

Margo Brown Miller 1989

On the drive to visit Paul's parents, Tamla decided to talk with mom and dad about college.

She began by saying this, "about college, I've given it a lot of thought and right now I haven't decided what I want to do in life. With that said, I would like to postpone it for a few years."

She braced for the worst, but instead got this from dad. "Sounds like you've thought this through and we just want to support you in whatever you want to do."

Then mom said "what do you want to do before going to college?"

Now she would explain what she wanted to do. Tamla was not too surprised but still thought there would be some resistance to her not going to school. The next thing she said was "I am so grateful to have this life, also to be an Indigo child, and part of the Gen X generation. With what you have both taught me about giving and receiving, I am ready to start giving."

Mom then said "that's wonderful dear. What do you have in mind?"

"I've been looking at The Peace Corps and doing that for a few years."

They both then nodded in the affirmative and dad said "please don't tell your grandparents today, let us do that."

The next year the High Council went into session and celebrated the Berlin Wall being destroyed.

Ambrosia spoke "this is a wonderful time for us and our people on Earth, to see such a hateful landmark be destroyed. Let's meditate and give thanks for this achievement." All motioned in the affirmative.

After the meditation was complete Terames said "I have an announcement to make."

Ambrosia nodded to Leto who said "please continue Terames with your announcement."

"As you know, Margo is beginning to take a leadership role in more areas of her life. Well, Tamla is now considering joining The Peace Corps for a few years, after finishing high school."

Ambrosia said "that is wonderful news she will gain much experience helping other people."

Ringo then said "I look for the day when all the families on

Earth are more like the Miller's. They're not perfect but they do try hard and are as one."

Ambrosia then said "Terames, Ringo, and Leto we need to make sure this family has help on their journeys."

The three got together and Terames being a chief said "we will go and spend tomorrow in the Orion conference room and devise our plan for this."

Both Ringo and Leto gave her the equivalent of a military salute to acknowledge her order to them.

She is coming home after three years of being in The Peace Corps, the only time Tamla would write would be to send some photographs of Africa, and the work she was doing over there. Once a week she would be with her parents in their dreams and with their Guides. Because they see her in their dreams, they are proud of her, but don't really miss her that much.

Margo's brother wasn't married, and Paul had no siblings, so Tamla was the only grandchild in both families. She was planning this big day and while talking with Paul she said "you are taking care of the plane tickets for my daddy and brother right?"

He walked up from behind and hugged her, then said "yes, Chief Margo." He started calling her this because of the learning she received from her mom.

A laugh from her, because so is ticklish "thank you dear, you are so good to me."

They invited the rebels to join them because this was a special day. Paul introduced them all to his parents and in-laws. He talked with his friends and was so happy to see Jenny and Cory together. They were all so pleased with Tamla and her friend Shasha couldn't wait to spend time with her.

Paul said "I'll see you guys later, I'm going to check on my parents." He then walked over to his parents and said "mom, dad, I want to tell you something that I've wanted to tell you for some time now."

His dad said "go ahead son, what is it?"

"Well when I was growing up as a boy, mom, you would teach me things you learned from Susan, and those were very good things. When I went to college I had a dream that seemed so real. Now to make a long story short, your friend Susan would have these dreams and would be taught by a Guide from the Pleiades. Well, that night her Guide became mine because I am one of 144,000 on this Earth that came here from the Pleiades, to help prepare our people for the changes that are coming."

Lucille understood what he said but dad had no idea. Paul Sr. said "son, I have no idea what you're talking about. You have made me proud with being a husband, father, and doctor. I'm sure there is something special about you."

Mom said "dad's busy with his stuff but I would like to know more about this. Especially with Susan gone, I miss her, and would like you to share more about her Guide."

"Will do mom, Margo is a Wayshower too, and your granddaughter is an Indigo child. This I will explain later."

Dad said "look Connor's over there. I'm going to go over and talk with him."

The Tamla welcome party was a success and all enjoyed getting together and meeting new people. Tamla and Shasha were the happiest.

A few days later Paul skipped his golf outing that day and went over to visited his mom. "Hi mom, how are you doing today?"

As she opened the door she said "fine son, what's the occasion?"

"Well, we are going to talk about the Pleiadians, and who they are." He told her about their dreams and how they would all be together. Most importantly he told her about how he was taught by his Guide Ringo and Amerorth from the moon base.

She was very receptive, she really liked the part about how Margo and Tamla would receive instruction from Margo's mom, who passed away some thirty years ago.

Blame it on CSPAN for airing the U S Congress live on TV, because that's what the girls started watching. Margo said to Tamla "can you believe he said that? He needs to spend some time with the High Council, they'd set him straight."

"I know mom, where do these people come from?"

Margo chuckled and said "from all over, I guess."

"Something needs to change in our government. After spending three years overseas, I expected better from my country." Then three days later, Margo and Tamla had something to tell Paul.

It's Friday night, they will be with their guides, and the girls made an agreement this night, that before going to sleep they would each ask Terames and Ringo to take them to the Council for an announcement. During their dream Paul said "we're at the High Council and it looks like something is happening tonight."

Ringo looked over at Terames and shook his head in the affirmative. Paul looked over at his girls and asked "do you two know what's going on?" They both shook their heads yes.

Ambrosia stood up and made an announcement "tonight is a very special night. One of our Wayshowers has decided to enter into human government." The whole Council stood and anticipated who that would be. Ambrosia then called on Terames "Terames would you please give the declaration."

She stood up and said "yes Your Grace, I want to call up my daughter and granddaughter." Paul knew who it was when Ambrosia called on Terames.

Their breakfast table was abuzz with excitement. Paul asked them "when did you make this decision and who was responsible for it?"

Margo pointed to Tamla and said "let your daughter tell you."

Tamla sipped her tea and smiled. He looked at her and said "well."

"Mom and I have been watching Congress on CSPAN for several months now, and we would listen to what they would say about legislations. Then a few days ago mom was telling me what needs to be done, how these people need to be educated by the High Council, and I always agreed with her and said, mom you need to run for congress."

They set up their campaign headquarters in town and she officially registered her name to run for the U. S. House of Representatives seat. Paul would be a major fund raiser and Tamla her Chief of Staff. Margo was so excited to use all this knowledge her mom had been teaching her all these years.

Later than evening Margo reflected on all that was happening, how her family, and friends were there to support her. Sipping some tea she wrote this poem to help her remember the things that her mom had taught her.

True Leadership

To be a leader is not a desire,
you can become one tested by fire.

It's not a matter of weak or strong,
if you aren't one, you're not wrong.

Leaders judge only from their heart,
treat all people as one is a good start.

Manage all resources with care,
mother earth will judge us fair.

Time has come to impart my knowledge,
this comes from the stars and not college.

Please open your hearts to me,
lighting the way for me to see.

Margo Brown Miller 1993

CHAPTER 15

Margo was very scared and nervous about this undertaking. Other than her travels on Friday nights to another galaxy, and the trip to Mt. Shasta, her life was not very complicated. Now there's Tamla, after three years in The Peace Corps, she on the other hand was a bundle of energy, and confidence.

The Miller headquarters was open for business and so Tamla called her first meeting. "Okay people we have a lot of work ahead of us and we need to recruit some volunteers." Grandma Lucille raised her hand then Tamla looked at her and said "yes grandma."

"You mean other than us four?"

Tamla smiled and said "I love you grandma, and yes we need more than four people."

Dad said "I'm going to make some fliers and post them

around town. Also we need to bring our candidate by to see Dorothy."

Some calls came in a couple of days after the fliers were posted. Tamla would take one very important call "hello, Margaret Miller for Congress headquarters. How may I be of service to you?"

The person on the other line said "yes I would like to know how I can help Mrs. Miller."

"Thank you we need all kinds of help, since this is our first time. Please come down to our headquarters when you can, we are here Monday thru Friday 9 until 6."

"Okay, my name is Jackie Williams and I'll be there today at 2 pm."

It was Wednesday, dad's day off from work, and they all went to lunch. Paul said "dad what do you think about this campaign so far?"

"Well son, we just started, but I think it's going great! Reminds me of your granddad the Senator and how much work that was. It's sad that those people are long gone."

Tamla said "so true grandpa, but we are going to do this, and the help will come pouring in soon."

Margo and Lucille both looked at each other and raised their tea cups and said together "that's our girl."

Its two o'clock and Ms. Jackie Williams arrived at their headquarters. Tamla sees her walk in and said to her "Hello you must be Ms. Williams."

She was an elderly woman who looked to be so kind that you just wanted to talk with her. "Yes and are you Ms. Tamla, I suppose?"

"Yes mam, that's me."

As they sat down Tamla learned that Jackie had worked some thirty years ago on a local campaign staff in the sixties. She was the Chief of Staff for that successful campaign. The week went by and they added two more people and their campaign was in full swing.

It's Friday night, the Miller family are asking to be brought to the Council, to ask Terames and Ambrosia questions about what to do next. After Tamla hugs grandma, Margo said "mom we need your help."

Terames smiled and then said "my dear didn't a Jackie Williams show up?"

With a tear of galactic magnitude she said "yes she did, thanks mom" and they were then given more information before they awoke in the morning.

During these next several months, the Margaret Brown Miller campaign received more help from the people on Earth, and especially a lot of guidance from above.

Paul was first chosen to be the other candidate for their practice debate, until Jackie said "this will not work and for many reasons. Just for starters what does Dr. Miller know about politics outside of the medical profession, and also I don't believe he can sling the mud at his wife."

Paul shook his head yes, and then Tamla said "Ms. Jackie how about you do it?"

"Thanks dear, but I can only advise you, but I don't have the strength to forcefully challenge Margo."

Tamla looked around and then picked someone, she said "Shasha, you are a law student and you have a lot of political knowledge. I think you should give it a try."

"Yes I will, but I don't fit the profile of the other candidate."

Jackie laughed and said "true, but you are a good choice."

Shasha did an excellent job, helping to prepare Margo for the upcoming debate. Jackie's knowledge was instrumental in the preparation, and Tamla learned a lot from her.

An official debate was scheduled at Auburn and there the gauntlet was thrown down. "Good evening fellow Alabamians, tonight we are going to find out about these two candidates" said the announcer.

Mr. Boyer won the toss and said "Mrs. Miller I being a southern gentleman, defer the opening remarks to you my lady."

She did a traditional curtsy and said "why thank Mr. Boyer, you sir are a gentleman."

Her remarks were mostly positive. In them she explained how our federal government can do a better job in equal rights for its citizens per the fourteenth amendment to the Constitution.

Well that's not how he returned the favour. He looked at the audience, rolled his eyes while she spoke, and then said "Mrs. Miller, are you that Pollyanna to think that it's that easy? I don't know where you've been these last twenty years but, I've been fighting for these rights all along."

She then smiled and said "Mr. Boyer sir, I raised my family and lived in this world outside of the beltway of Washington, D.C. It seems that you don't understand that the people aren't looking for the government to give them anything. They want it to act as though it was one of them and not some high-minded, not well educated in life elitist like you." The crowd went wild with applause.

Hours before all the final votes were counted, the Miller headquarters were ready to celebrate.

Tamla called a meeting. The place was packed and she said "this is an historic day, we feel confident that our candidate will win tonight. She will not only represent us here, but the entire state of Alabama."

The people cheered and chanted "Margo, Margo."

Tamla was standing next to Shasha and held her hand as the votes were being tallied.

The High Council was in session watching the votes being given in the United States this November 2nd, 1994. They had several Wayshowers running for office that evening. Ambrosia said "today is a major step in the direction that the planet earth will be guided in the future. We need to make sure she gets all the support from us that we possibly can give her. Thank you and goodnight beautiful blue planet earth."

She served her country well for four terms and turning 56 she missed her home in Alabama. Like most people this was a time in life to start travelling the world and there are a lot of spiritual sites they want to visit.

With Tamla as her Chief of Staff, Shasha as her Deputy Chief, and Head Legal Counsel, these girls were now ready to make big changes in this world together.

At their home in Georgetown Tamla and Shasha were contemplating what they wanted to do next.

Tamla said "Shasha, sweetheart let's ask our moms during dinner tonight what they feel our next steps should be."

"Honey I agree, somehow I can feel another new campaign

starting."

Tamla laughed and kissed her and said "do you think we're ready to face the homophobes now?"

"Damn straight they need to wake-up and be challenged."

Dinner and an evening on the Potomac was where the plan began. What a group of powerful women they were; Margo, Jenny, Tamla, and Shasha. This dinner would be the equivalent of the Jekyll Island Club meeting. We'll leave it at that for now.

Tamla began the conversation and said "mom, Mrs. Greene, Shasha and I have been talking about what we want to do next. Do either of you have any thoughts on this?"

Margo said "yes we do. We were talking about going home to Alabama and then wondered what you two would want to do next. There is a lot of legislation still pending and some needing to be started. With the coalition that we have put together we feel it would be detrimental to not at least leave them in good hands."

Tamla couldn't agree more and she gave a very low sounding applause. So it's settled, the moms are going home, and the girls are going to continue what they started eight years ago.

Margo spent some quiet time at home on the farm. She reflected on how much she missed her new adopted home of Alabama. Indiana was always going to be her first love, since she was born there and that was where she spent many days with her mom. This morning she made a pot of tea and grabbed her notebook. Out the door and to the lake she went. Once she located the gazebo that was were her destination would end. Comfortable with her tea on the table and notebook in hand she wrote this.

The Call

Our being resides in this body very well,
just like a sea creature in a shell.

We control movement by our spirit,
the galaxy responds when we steer it.

To say we create all that's shown,
is to acknowledge truth that's known.

To lead my people is an honor,
just like my daddy named Connor.

I've served these many years
and there have been many tears.

Some have even sent people to die,
for this has made my spirit cry.

This writing I know is long,
I should have written it as a song.

That was not said as a joke,
nor was it merely written to poke.

I wish our laws could be rhymed,
we could reach the conscious mind.

Love and light to you all,
I now step down from this call.

Honourable Margo Brown Miller 2002

CHAPTER 16

Margo and Paul had talked about this for years, well decades that is. Now that she was back on the farm in Alabama they know it's time to travel. They're on the front porch and he says to her "our dear Tamla sure grew to be a fine person, and now that her life is on course, I suppose we need to decide what we want to do next."

She took a deep breath of that fall night air and said "true so true, let's travel the world!"

There were a few things to tidy up first. It was Friday night and they had some questions to ask their Guides.

Paul said "Darling before we turn in tonight let's ask Terames and Ringo about travelling the world."

"Good idea we will have Tamla there with us in our dream, so we can make a plan without having to fly to D.C."

He smiled and said "that is a great thing we have in these dreams."

This time Terames was the first to greet them "hello my children this is a special time for our visit. There are some big changes coming. We will need to go to the High Council to receive instructions on what is to happen next."

Paul then said to Ringo "I suppose you received our request?"

"Oh yes we did and this plan was already in the works."

Tamla looked a little confused. Then Margo said "dear we wanted to tell you tonight what this was about."

Terames looked at Ringo and said "let's get them to the Council, they are waiting."

Ambrosia was very pleased with this family and tonight they were going to know that. Terames stood up and reported to Ambrosia "Your Grace we have brought the Miller family here as you requested."

"Thank you Chief, now let's get to business. Tamla you have taken your moms place in the Congress and with help from Shasha, I'm sure you will continue to do a fine job there. Now Paul you will need to take a few years off from your practice so you and Margo can go travel. You both will travel to the seven key energy vortices of the planet. There you will gain more energy through your Chakra's and cleanse them for your next mission. You both will receive instructions from your Guides. Mt Shasta has already been visited, so you have six to do."

They just looked at each other and then awoke. The next morning at breakfast Paul asked Margo "what do you think Ambrosia meant by travel?"

"I'm not sure, but it does sound like its big, I mean she said you will need to take a few years off from your practice."

"True, we will need to find someone to look after the farm and you know my parents are too old to do that anymore."

She said "I'm sure someone will be provided, remember when Ambrosia speaks, things tend to fall into place." Paul just grinned.

It wasn't three days later and they received a call. She answered "Hello this is Margo."

I know most people don't answer the phone like that, but after eight years in the Capitol, that's how she did it, although she did drop the *honorable* part.

"Margo, this is Jenny, how are you doing?"

"Fine, are you and Cory doing okay?"

"We're great, we are moving to your area soon. Cory has an opportunity to manage an auto shop." Margo knew that this was an opportunity for them all.

Now the Greene's are coming to watch the farm for the next few years. Paul and Margo were set to travel and tonight they got their first destination.

Paul said "Hello Ringo, now where are Terames, Tamla and Shasha?"

"Paul, Margo, you will be visiting with me for the next few years, and occasionally going to the High Council. You will visit them there when you report to Ambrosia on your journey. Terames will be helping Tamla as she did for you Margo when you were in the Congress."

Margo laughed and said "okay, it's all planned out I see."

Ringo then gave them their first destination and the next morning Margo wrote something very telling.

Embrace Life

Life is the journey we are on,
don't be afraid when it's gone.

It's full of things to be learned,
don't spend your time being concerned.

Just like the flower that flourishes,
we gravitate to the light which nourishes.

Embark on a journey every day,
then let your spirit find the way.

I'm leaving the astral travel for a time,
and to give this body something to rhyme.

This music comes from the Earth,
this blessed planet of my birth.

Margo Brown Miller 2007

Paul read her poem and said "your writing gets better with time. I'm taking this one with us on our journey."

She walked over to him and said "open up your arms!" He just received a huge hug from the writer.

Paul sighed and said "let's go to our travel agent and get our trip to Peru planned."

At Lake Titicaca, their first stop for the second chakra. Paul was so excited he opened his arms and said "beautiful planet, this is a special place to be."

Margo only said "let me catch my breath first."

The climb was worth the view of this pristine lake at

12,500 feet. Well at least they climbed quite a bit of it that day.

Paul said "dear we will be here for a few months so just enjoy."

She walked over to him and put her arm around his waist and said "give me a high altitude kiss."

Their plan was to visit all six islands on the lake and then go to Machu Picchu. But tonight they are going to have some new visitors in their dreams.

"Ringo, where are we going tonight?" Paul said as their visit began.

Ringo chuckled, then looked at Margo, and said "to your favorite place, the moon base."

She smiled and said "Ringo, this will make his night."

Traveling to the base they were surprised. Paul and Margo were startled by some fellow Earthlings. Paul asked "who are these people, they look to be from hundreds of years ago?"

Ringo answered "you are correct, these people are Incas from the past. They have already crossed over and tonight they inhabited these replica bodies they were in before."

Margo then spoke "are they going to teach us in their old ways?"

"Margo you are very perceptive."

They awoke with their spirits riding high and a sense of belonging to the area they were in.

A few months later while visiting Machu Picchu, Paul was interested in the sites, but mostly the energies around them. Margo grabbed his hand and said "walk with me, my best friend, and galactic companion all these years."

Paul said "my Angel you have a wonderful way with words."

She smiled and said "they are what built this universe." This was good for her to clear the entropy of government she dealt with for eight years. Now they have energized their second chakra and it was time to move on.

After a night with the High Council to give their report on their second Chakra, Paul and Margo enjoyed their visit with Terames and Tamla.

After waking up Paul said at breakfast "I know we have a lot of life left, but sometimes I am amazed at how great it's all been. We have gone from meeting at Woodstock to going to Mt. Shasta and then to Washington DC to now leaving Peru on our way to Australia. Not to mention our nightly visits to the dark side of the moon, or the Pleiades to meet with the High Council, all simply unbelievable."

Margo shook her head and said "imagine being told this almost 40 years ago?"

Time was to be spent here in the Northern Territory of Australia, commonly known as Ayers Rock. The mission was to meet with the locals, mostly Aboriginal people, and learn about this third chakra area. After getting there, which was a long trip and getting settled in Paul said "wow the middle of nowhere."

Margo laughed and said "I'm sure after we leave this place we'll want to come back again."

"Maybe so, it's different that's for sure."

This was to help emotions, since the third chakra is from the solar plexus. They spent about four months there and then gave their report to the Council. Mostly Ambrosia wanted to make sure they were achieving the goals that were set out for them.

On the flight back to Alabama for a couple of months to refresh, Margo leaned her seat back reflected on their recent travels and wrote.

Love All People

Meeting indigenous people where they live,
will surely make one's spirit want to give.

I'm lucky to travel on this road,
love's the greatest gift to be bestowed.

So be happy where you are,
continue to sparkle like a star.

Mother earth your love is so dear,
bless me on my journey while I'm here.

Margo Brown Miller 2008

Next stop will be England and they are excited about that. "Paul it says here that we are going to where the Holy Grail might be."

"Yes dear, crop circles, Stonehenge, and much more."

Now Paul was excited and they would spend several months on the island. This was for the fourth chakra and it dealt with the heart. Glastonbury will be their first stop and then to Shaftesbury. This would be a great visit for them.

On the plane again where Margo said "wow that seven

months went fast."

Paul agreed and said "the pyramids of Egypt what a great thing to see."

This is the fifth chakra and it deals with the throat or voice. They will see the great pyramids, and travel to Mt. Sanai and then to Israel to visit those sites. A lot of energy here too and after a few months they won't want to leave there either.

They went back to the Council in this dream, and spent time with Tamla and Terames. Margo ran to Tamla and hugged her, then said "my daughter, we've missed you. How are you girls doing?"

She kissed her and said "mom, the religious right have shifted from worrying about flag burning to keeping us from getting married. I wish they had more to do with their time, they should want to help the inner cities in this country, before they explode with violence."

"Okay dear, I see that our congressional seat is in good hands."

Paul then gave their report to Ambrosia and Terames. And then back on a plane to Alabama for a few weeks before going on to the next site.

The next two stops would finish their three year journey. The first was for the sixth chakra which is for the pineal gland or 'third eye'. They would travel to Western Europe and meditate to open this and recognize other dimensions. The last stop is Mt. Kailas in the Himalayas, there they would spend this time to develop the consciousness of their seventh chakra which is the crown, and it is right above your head. They would spend time with the Tibetan people and visit with the monks.

On the final connected flight to Alabama, Paul and Margo couldn't shake the beauty of Mt. Kailas, at over 21,000 feet, and the monasteries they visited.

Paul said "beautiful places and yet the most beautiful thing of it all was the people."

"That is so true."

She took a nap, and when she awoke it was dark, and the stars were twinkling while they flew over the ocean. Looking around her, everyone was asleep even her wonderful man, who she thought hung the moon. The night seemed to call out for her to write, and put her feelings of the last three years down.

A Spiritual Journey

Mt. Shasta is a site to behold,
experience it firsthand and not be told.

Titicaca Lake at over 12,000 feet,
your heart will want to skip a beat.

Machu Picchu can't be explained,
stones placed that way and still remain?

Ayers Rock stands so big and strong,
to guard our spirit from all that's wrong.

A visit to England to search for the Grail,
leaves some grand stories needed to tell.

The time on the Isles did touch my heart,
and the kinship that was my start.

The Pyramids are so huge for the eye to see,
structures that big is unbelievable to be.

Castles and history ruled by the stirrup,
we even travelled by horse in Western Europe.

Mt. Kailas is so high to be found,
it's the seventh chakra of the crown.

From these places energy will come,
hearts are the rivers they are from.

Margo Brown Miller 2010

CHAPTER 17

To say nothing happened in 2012 is an understatement. There were plenty of things that happened that year and a few years before and after. Lots of doomsday predictions, movies, and books were everywhere.

Coming back from town Paul said "why all the negativity about this year? The Mayans didn't predict that, it was just an end of an Earth cycle."

Margo just shook her head and said "I know, you think they want these tragedies or else why give into it."

"Yea, you're right the negativity today seems greater than in 1987 and far worse than in 1969. There were so many bad things happening in 1969 but we were still positive."

She sighed and said "I'm not sure why, but it does seem that way. Maybe people are bored with all the doomsday predictions and can't think positive thoughts?"

They spent the rest of the day just reminiscing about their

trip to Mt. Shasta for the Harmonic Conversion of 1987. Margo said to Paul "you know mom has been acting strangely lately. Reminds me of when they were ready to tell us about the harmonic conversion in 87."

It's Friday night and they are ready to enter dreamland, to discuss these things with their Guides, and daughter.

Paul said very jokingly "Ringo, how are you tonight?"

Ringo having fun said "just fine doctor, how about you and these two lovely ladies?"

Margo was amused and said "haven't heard him called doctor in many years."

Then Terames said "okay children enough of the fun, let's go visit Ambrosia and the Council tonight."

Tamla said "grandma you seem to be in a hurry, is everything okay?"

She smiled and said "everything is fine Sweetie we just have some new instructions to receive tonight."

The atmosphere seemed very hopeful that night, but they didn't know why.

Leto greeted them in the usual way "welcome Wayshowers we have been expecting you."

Then Ambrosia laughed, it seemed her joy was hard to contain tonight.

Paul spoke up and said "okay, what's going on tonight? Then he noticed his fellow Wayshowers named the Rebels were there too"

Leto whispered to Ambrosia and said "we have many things to cover tonight." Then turned and said "First Paul and Margo, you have achieved your next level of accession, and you will be informed about your next journey."

It was quiet for a time and then Paul said "the next journey and what will that be?"

The next journey was to be told by Ambrosia, who then said. "Paul, Margo, and Tamla, this one will involve you three, and help from the Rebels. There are still 144,000 Wayshowers on the earth and the world's population has doubled since the last ones arrived. What we need you to do is, to start assuming leadership positions in government. This will allow you to start making changes to prepare the people for the new Earth to come." A couple of deep breaths and then they awoke.

Well a trip to Washington D.C. and then to plan a conference with the Rebels at the farm. The place had really grown over the years, there was a guesthouse of some twelve rooms, fully furnished and stocked.

It was Spring break for the Congress, and Paul and Margo, decided to drive up there. First stop was Atlanta and that's where Paul surprised her.

"Oh Paul it's the motel we stayed at in 1969"

He said "yes and we are going for coffee tonight by the creek." This brought back some very pleasant memories for them.

Beautiful Georgetown is where their daughter lived with her partner Shasha. They arrived just before noon and since they stayed the night in Richmond the drive wasn't that long. The door opens and a sweet little six year old girl is standing there in front of Shasha.

Margo smiles and says "and who are you, an Angel maybe?"

She laughed and turned to hug Shasha. Shasha hugs her

and says "come in we've been expecting you."

Paul drops their bags and said "where's Tamla?"

"She had to go into the Capitol for some business this morning. She will meet us for lunch on the river at two."

Paul was upstairs unloading the bags when Margo asked "okay who is this little Angel girl?"

"We are waiting on the papers to adopt her. She's been with us on the weekends for a few months now."

"What's your name little Angel?" Margo asked.

She smiled and said "Brenda is my name, what's yours?"

"You can call me grandma, if you like."

Brenda looked over at Shasha, and then Shasha nodded yes. Then quickly she took off and gave Margo a big hug, and said "you are now my grandma."

The Boathouse is one of Paul's favorite restaurants in Georgetown. The seafood is the best he's had, in this country that is. There he made sure that little Brenda sat right between him and Margo. A few minutes later Tamla arrived and their conversations went from getting caught up on politics to what about our last dream.

Tamla said "mom are you getting back into politics or is it dad's turn?"

"For one thing your daddy wants nothing to do with politics except to support us. Now with that said the governor's office looks to be wide open for 2014."

Shasha said "Mrs. Miller is that what you want to do?"

"Shasha, you can call me mom, and I think so. I've been out of it for ten years now and I'm ready to make some changes for my people of Alabama."

"Mom, I like calling you that, thank you. Mom you are an

inspiration to Tamla and I, and we want to read your new poems that you've written."

Later that night they both reflected on their next journey and Paul said "dear, Alabama is going to be blessed again with your leadership and compassion."

"Paul you are the wind beneath my wings."

He kissed her and said "I do hope that's not hot air."

Margo smiled and said "you silly man, goodnight." Then she wrote this.

Kind Heart

Prepare your people for the day,
follow your Heart it knows the way.

Teach them to Love one another,
because we are all sister, and brother.

The universe dances to vibrations,
tune in and feel these sensations.

Judgement and fear can never ride,
when we have Love and hope on our side.

Join us please and change your mind,
let your Heart guide you to be kind.

I'll close with this one thought,
know the new Earth can't be bought.

Margo Brown Miller 2013

The   Miller   headquarters   was   abuzz   at   home   in

Montgomery, the capitol of Alabama. The people of her state loved this Governor, and she was running for another term.

She made some big changes in the way the state was governed, in that she revised the tax laws with the help of the congress.

In one of her new campaign commercials she said "people of Alabama we together have made many positive changes these last four years. One of these changes we made was in the tax code. This was a way to participate and to help each other, therefore creating a spirit of one community."

Her challenger Patricia Newberry, knew that she didn't have a chance of winning the election, so she decided to campaign against Margo in a positive way.

In another one of her commercials she even said "Governor Miller has done a fine job of steering this state in a positive direction. When I was in the Senate I supported some 96% of her bills. If you elect me as Governor I would merely continue to follow the same path of co-operation between all of us that she laid out."

In the evening of the election she not only congratulated the Governor on winning again, but she gave her a big hug, and a wonderful speech praising her leadership.

Paul and Margo had been learning more about the "new Earth" that was coming. This night things seemed to change a bit.

Paul grabbed his girls' hands and said "where are we tonight?"

They looked around and didn't know for sure. Tamla said "it looks like a new Earth."

Margo said "ah, this is what we've been studying here these last few months."

Then seemingly from nowhere they heard "welcome to the new Earth." They looked above them, and on a cloud were Terames, and Ringo.

Paul then said "maybe we've been here before and it seemed more like a dream then."

Ringo blurted out "you sir are correct, this is going to be your new home one day."

They were speechless, until Terames asked them "well, what do you think?"

Margo looked and said "mom it is a beautiful place, probably the way it was eons ago."

"Yes, that is true."

Paul asked her "what are we supposed to do here?"

"Well Paul, that is a good question and there is a long answer but, mainly you are one of many that will inhabit this Earth first." They just looked around and then woke up.

Margo addressed her family that morning during breakfast and said "okay we've been shown our heavenly home to come. We need to remember that we don't know the day that this will happen, so we need to stay focused on the job at hand."

Tamla, Shasha and, Brenda were visiting for the Christmas break, so Tamla looked over at her family, and said "you are right mom, Shasha and I are now parents and Brenda is our priority." Paul just sat there and enjoyed listening to the girls plan it all out.

Tamla and Shasha were legally married in 2016, shortly after the Supreme Court declared same-sex marriage to be made legal on June 26, 2015.

Now that the girls have gone back up to Georgetown, the Miller's, and Greene's where spending the day together.

Paul asked them "have you two been having any dreams about a new Earth?"

Cory said "yes we have and we were going to ask you the same thing. Is the place pristine and were you told we were going to inhabit it first?"

Margo said "yes exactly."

Then Jenny said "it's beautiful but a little disturbing, in that we aren't given the date that this is to happen."

Love's Horizon

The new horizon is there for you,
to inherit a new Earth that's green and blue.

Live the life you've been given now,
with courage that you've always known how.

Love all Spirits and teach them,
so they will sparkle like a gem.

You will sparkle like the stars above,
and there is no power greater than Love.

Help each other and be a blessing,
for doing this is extremely professing.

Margo Brown Miller 2019

CHAPTER 18

Paul looked at his beautiful wife of all these years and thought *I am so lucky to have her love for eternity.* He then breathed in all the good he was feeling.

In some ways it was like having an unfair advantage, but then again it could also drive a person crazy to live in two different worlds.

Paul was studying about some of the new synthetic bodies that were being created on the present Earth. He wanted to be taken to the moon base tonight to ask Amerorth some questions. Ringo was there to greet him, so Paul asked "are we going to the moon base tonight?"

"Yes we are, and the girls are going to the Council to converse with Ambrosia, and Terames."

On the base Paul quickly found Amerorth and said "buddy I've got some questions for you tonight."

"Okay, they are about DNA, I suppose."

"Yes they are, the scientists in the medical community are using DNA to splice genes to create bodies to inhabit."

"We knew this was going to happen and they will be used in the future."

"What does that mean, in the future?" He didn't receive an answer and then woke up and wrote this.

Being trapped in this life of time, it is understood that people would attempt to extend it. New bodies are being made to achieve this goal. However so far the best we can do is replace a limb or an organ. Even though these bodies are synthetically created and have a longer life span, they still will break down over time. The problem is our Spirit cannot inhabit these "temples made with hands" therefore we should look more to a heavenly eternal life.

Dr. Paul Miller 2019

This was a big day for the Governor of Alabama. Today the President of the United States was giving her an award. Paul was there and so was his mom, the Greene's, Congresswoman Tamla Miller-Greene, Shasha and Brenda.

When the whole ceremony began, Paul was so proud of this strong hearted woman from Indiana that he met some fifty years ago. Margo was instructed to approach the President and receive her medal. Then the President said "thank you for serving your country, state and party with honor these many years."

Margo gathered her composure and then while shaking her hand said "thank you Mr. President, you are an inspiration to me and this country."

Later that day they were having dinner on the Potomac

and Paul asked Brenda "well I suppose you will want to follow after your mom's and your grandma into politics right?"

Turning fourteen this year was the time to start thinking about what you wanted to do in this life.

"Grandpa, I have been thinking more about being a doctor like you. I've actually been reading a lot about being a Cardiologist." Both Tamla and Shasha looked at him and just smiled.

He then said "girls she will need to spend her summers with us then." They both agreed.

A couple of months later Margo had announced her retirement from politics. She and Paul were turning seventy-four, and they thought it best to concentrate their energy on family, and friends. Their dreams where becoming longer it seemed, tonight they would visit the High Council first, and receive their next journey.

Ringo and Terames brought them straight to Ambrosia. Who said "tonight I will impart to you both your next assignment".

They were then given the assignment of traveling to this new Earth and working with other Wayshower's to start setting it up for the inhabitants of the current Earth's third dimension.

Ambrosia told Margo "you dear are to be a Chief on this new Earth and Paul you will be a Chief Mystical Physician there."

Margo said to Ambrosia "it would be an honor to follow in my mother's footsteps."

That evening her daddy was there, he had crossed over many years before. She gave him a hug and told him how much she loved him. Paul's dad had crossed over a few years later but he was still involved in doing his life review.

Paul woke up and said to Margo "wow, we sure have some wonderful work to do."

She kissed him and said "right alongside you my dear husband."

She was so happy to see her daddy again, it had been many years. They knew that today was the first day to start preparing for their eventual departure and today Paul was going to the college to start getting all the information needed to plan Brenda's entrance into Auburn medical school.

Aspire to be

The autumn of your life,
brings with it some strife.

Embrace it for now,
time has come to see how.

In this galaxy you can grow,
to be an actor in its show.

The challenge is then given,
as one and not to be riven.

I will continue my role on a new Earth,
and this time it's for an eternal birth.

Doing this with my twin flame by my side,
makes this a joyous occasion to ride.

I close with this burning thought,
aspire to be all that will be wrought.

Margo Brown Miller 2022

Ringo was there with Paul and he noticed him looking at the night sky and searching in it. "Paul what are you looking for?"

"The moon base, is it a part of the new Earth?"

"I should have known you would have asked that. You will have something better here, and you will see your friend Amerorth soon. First let's go and start getting acclimated to your new 'Wizards castle."

Paul looked at him and said "really?"

"Well, it will be whatever you make of it."

No trip to the High Council tonight except for Tamla. She would be with Ambrosia from now on, except on an occasional visit with the family on the new Earth.

Margo was talking with her mom and asked her "are we going to pattern the government here after Earth or the Pleiades?"

"Good question we would like to do a little of both, since we are patterning our new bodies, and living after our time on the Earth. Tonight I want you to start getting acclimated to governing here with your fellow Wayshowers."

"Okay mom, I'm so glad you are here to help me."

Margo spent some time getting to know the other Wayshowers that would be leading the new Earth government. While she was doing this, Paul was reading and studying all the books from the great libraries through-out history on Earth, and in the galaxy. He was amazed at the speed he could read and retain this information.

They still retained their five senses and gained a couple more, but they were starting to get hungry. Paul said to Ringo "man I've never been hungry in one of these dreams before."

Ringo said "Let's go find Margo and Terames and eat."

"Good idea, you lead the way my friend."

Upon finding the girls, Paul walked up to Margo and she said "let's eat."

"Okay where?"

Then Terames and Ringo smiled at each other and she said "they are in for a treat."

Travel in the new Earth was by any means you wanted to go. They chose to simply fly to their destination. With Ringo and Terames leading the way they flew over some beautiful green mountains that had the most blueish lakes you ever seen.

Margo said to Paul "these dreams are getting better each time."

He smiled, squeezed her hand, and said "so do you my Love."

It didn't take long and actually there is no time on the new Earth, so it was just a beautiful journey. They were seated by a lake, and the table was a huge flat mushroom, and they sat suspended in the air. The food came out and was put on the table. It was mostly fruits and vegetables, nothing strange looking, but nothing cooked either.

Paul noticed an apple and took a bite and then said "OMG, this is delicious!"

Terames handed Margo a carrot and said "try this dear."

Margo looked at it, then took a bite, and then she chewed it and said "that carrot was great, starting with the crunch!"

Ringo just laughed and said "you guys are going to love living here."

Shortly after they ate, Ringo and Terames took their guests

to one of the many vertical oceans.

Paul looked at Margo and said "I wish Tamla was here to enjoy the dolphins."

"Yes, I will always remember our little girl swimming with them her first time."

Terames hugged them both and said "go enjoy your time with them."

Paul smirked and said "last one in is a rotten egg!"

When they dove into the water they then lost all ability to talk with their mouths, but communication just went on at a higher level.

Margo said "look, Paul one of Tamla's dolphin friends. I think she called her "Blue Fin" because of her dark blue fin."

Blue Fin answered "you are right Margo. Hello to you both."

They both woke about the same time and Margo said "dear that was a long dream, wasn't it?"

"Yes it was, what do you want to do today? I have a thought for you."

She looked at him and said "I want to play some golf."

"I love it when you read my mind." Normally that is true, but today she really wanted to play some golf.

"Paul, this is true but today, I want to smell the air, walk on the grass, and look at the lakes, while I exercise my body."

"I'll get the clubs and we'll do nine and lunch at the clubhouse before finishing the back nine."

Later that evening Margo wrote this.

Judgement

Know that your mind tries to control,
control all your thoughts and your soul.

Love all and don't ever give in,
you know Love is found from within.

Look at every creature you create,
now open your Heart and celebrate.

Change your mind from desire,
and let your Heart lift you higher.

Your eyes will now see that the Earth,
is a beautiful planet that's full of worth.

Learn to live in Love and not hate,
reside in your Heart before it's too late.

Caring for others is good for your soul,
it breaks up the reigns of mind control.

Do good it will only make you strong,
inside Spirit knows right from wrong.

To live a lifetime you see many things,
now I want all that true Love brings.

Margo Brown Miller 2023

Tamla had a special guest in her dream tonight.

She said "Ambrosia, how are you doing this evening?"

"Simply wonderful and I have some special guests here for you tonight."

Tamla looked around and said "who, I don't see anyone new, that I know?"

Ambrosia said "come on out girls."

Tamla's jaw dropped when she saw Shasha and Brenda walk out from behind Ambrosia.

CHAPTER 19

There are many ways that the people on planet Earth are separated. With renewable, clean, and free energy available, the economies of the world had to adjust. At first many people panicked, and this helped cause their own demise. Luckily there were some people, about 144,000 that just seemed to have the answers. These Wayshowers were mostly in positions of leadership throughout the world. Luckily for the world they were there to help guide the planet into this new era.

Their sweet little Angel is now ready to go to college. She asked her moms, if she could live with grandpa, and grandma while she attended Auburn medical school.

"You're going to let her drive your dad's old Fleetline?" Margo asked Paul.

"You know it, why wait until she graduates. I might not be around then."

Margo just laughed and said "you old kook, you're not going anywhere without me." But first they were going to pick her up at the airport in it.

Margo and Paul both will turn seventy-eight this year and they understand that their time is limited in this form. Brenda was talking with Margo, she told her about how she is in the same dreams of her moms, and Margo was pleased to hear this. Paul was walking by and Margo called him "darling come over here."

"What's up?"

"Did you know that the girls are in the same dreams together?"

"Yes I did sorry, Tamla told me that, and I forgot all about it."

Brenda asked "what does that mean?"

They were told over half a century ago that they could request something from their Guides before dreaming. Well tonight was Friday and they were ready to ask them.

Margo said "after dinner tonight let's all drink some herbal tea on the porch."

All agreed and after dinner they would sit on the porch. Brenda had a couple of weeks before going to Auburn, so they thought it better to prepare her.

Margo said "here's the tea". They were all seated and she looked at Paul to start the conversation, and he did.

"Brenda, we are so proud of you for making great grades, and being accepted into medical college, especially our alma mater."

Margo was good with that and then said "dear we need to let you in on a family secret."

"What is that grandma?"

Paul knew that Margo wanted him to carry the conversation so he answered her "you know about the dreams?"

"A little, I know that Shasha and I were in Tamla's dream, and she was at the High Council of the Pleiades."

Margo asked "how many dreams were you in?"

"Just a few dreams so far."

Then Paul didn't want to dance around this anymore and said "well your grandma and I have been sharing our dreams since 1969." Then he asked the ultimate question. "Were you given a Guide?"

"I don't think so."

"That's okay grandma and I are going to ask our Guides if you can join us in our dreams tonight."

"Wow, you can do that?"

Margo spoke and said "yes we can, did you meet your mom Tamla's Guide?"

"Yes her name is Ambrosia, I think."

"Have you met Terames?"

Brenda said "I don't think so."

"Angel, that's my mom Elizabeth, who went back to being Terames after she crossed over. Maybe you will meet her tonight."

Brenda didn't know what to say except for "cool, so cool."

That night they did ask their Guides if she could be in their dreams and of course the answer was yes.

Brenda said "mom, hey I'm back in your dream! Where's Shasha?"

"I don't know we'll have to ask Ambrosia." Before she could find her, she found some others, and said "mom, dad hey you're here tonight. Wait a minute, this isn't the High Council."

Margo said "right you are sweetie, this is the new Earth."

"New Earth, will Ambrosia be joining us?"

Paul said "I don't know, we've been coming here for a while now, and we haven't seen her yet. Honey what do you want to do tonight?"

Margo had the plan "I'll take Tamla, show her the new government, and you take Brenda to your Wizards castle."

Brenda clinched both her fists back and said "hell yeah, let's go grandpa!"

Later in the visit Terames showed up at the government center. "Mom, where have you been?" exclaimed Margo.

"I brought a friend."

Then Shasha came out from behind her and said "this place is pristine, oh hi Tamla darling."

Tamla ran over to her, gave her a hug and a kiss then said "I'm so glad you're here." They proceeded to learn about this new government with the idea of bringing some of it back to Washington, D.C.

Meanwhile Grandpa and granddaughter were in a library heaven. "Grandpa, this place is amazing!"

"Yes it is and one day we will all live here."

"I can't wait to use this library for school."

He had a thought, but instead said "wait a minute, you have to be careful what you share outside of your dreams. We don't want them coming after us with butterfly nets."

She laughed and said "you're right grandpa many people wouldn't understand a lot of this."

They all were getting hungry so Paul and Margo knew

what to do. Paul told Ringo "hey let's get with the others and eat."

Ringo smiled and said "do it, you know how to fly."

Paul looked at Brenda and said "are you ready to fly?"

She looked at him wide-eyed and said "you mean I can fly?" He took her by the hand and off they went.

Up in the sky flying, Paul and Brenda were on their way to where the others were. Looking up Shasha said "look, look Paul, and Brenda are flying right over here!"

Margo and Terames looked at each other and smiled. Terames said to Margo "wait till they taste the food."

Margo said "oh yeah."

Paul and Brenda landed and he said "let's go eat."

Then Tamla took Shasha by the hand, and off they went with the others, flying to one of their eating places. Just like Terames and Margo expected the girls couldn't believe how great the food tasted.

The next morning both of them had to be woken up. Brenda went to their door, knock, knock "Grandma, grandpa are you guys awake? I fixed breakfast, eggs and pancakes."

They looked at each other and then the clock on the wall, which said 10 am. Paul said "wow, that dream sure took a lot out of us."

Margo kissed him and said "good morning my Prince."

"Well good morning to you too, my beautiful lady."

Margo then grabbed her notebook to write after breakfast.

Brenda said "good morning you two. What, did you travel to a new Earth or something last night?"

Paul said "yum pancakes!"

Margo laughed and then said "Angel you were there too."

Brenda ran up to her and gave her a big hug. Brenda was full of questions about last night.

Paul said "we do this once a week and next time we go to the High Council we'll ask Ambrosia about your Guide."

Brenda then said "Ambrosia, I remember Ambrosia the High Counselor."

Margo said "you will be included for sure."

Both Paul and Brenda needed to go to the college and take care of some business today.

Margo went out to her gazebo and sat her pitcher of ice tea on the table and wrote.

Love's Wisdom

Today I feel like a fancy cat,
and I've often worn a different hat.

I am so happy of all these things,
that life is filled with Love and sings.

You know Love that can be found,
even in places where there is no sound.

This present Earth has been so true,
but now there is a new Earth for me and you.

Be patient and don't follow sadness,
because it will only lead you to madness.

Search in your Heart and it will show,
you all the answers that you need to know.

Hold steady and just believe,
give out good thus you will receive.

Being young in life can be confusing,
looking back and you see it was amusing.

Find pleasure in just being alone,
master yourself as a star to be shone.

Margo Brown Miller 2024

It seemed like yesterday for Margo, when she first saw this beautiful brown-eyed little Angel, standing in front of Shasha.

"Paul, dear we are so lucky to have lived such a wonderful life, and all along be aware of our eternal Spirit."

"Yes and I couldn't be any happier with how it's all turned out. The thing that's amazing to me is, how we are spending some of our evenings living in our new home planet, and working on setting it up for that day." With that said, she looked at him and smiled.

Now their little Angel has grown up and is in her third year of medical school.

"Grandma, let me help you cook dinner tonight."

"Brenda dear, you have school work to do."

She then put her book down and said "you are more important than that book."

Margo knew she couldn't refuse her and she loved having her help in the kitchen.

Paul walks in and says "yum, that sauce smells terrific and I'm starving." He's been out cutting the grass on this hot Alabama day.

At the table they discussed Brenda's school and Paul said "Brenda you haven't told us where you want to work when you graduate."

"Grandpa, that's apparent isn't it? Why else would I go to school here in Montgomery, I love this place."

"Ah so you mean the Jackson Hospital, Cardiology and Heart Center."

"Yes Grandpa, they are doing some wonderful things there."

Margo said "wonderful, we know you'll create some memories here just like we have."

That evening they were surprised with a dream where Paul said "Margo what's going on?"

"I don't know it looks like we are on the new Earth tonight."

Paul then looked around and there he spotted Ringo walking up. Seeing him too Ringo said "Hi my Wayshowers how are you tonight?"

"Ringo it's not Friday night?"

"I know that."

Paul imagined the Jeopardy music in his head, then laughed, and said "why are we here tonight?"

"You two are going to be coming here more often, you need to start weaning yourself from the third dimension."

Ringo walked over to them, took their hand, and said "let's go somewhere special tonight."

They then went up into the air and on to their destination. "This is it right down there" he said.

They landed and Margo said "these are homes."

"Yes they are, now you two go pick one out."

They both looked at each other and then she said "are we staying here for good?"

Anxiously Paul asked "are we?"

"Listen, you know the day is coming, but not tonight. We don't know when it is but, you do know it's near, so go find a house, and therefore over time get it the way you want it to be."

Paul laughed and told Margo "so Ringo is our realtor now?"

They found their home, not too big but enough rooms to have a couple of guests. Nice big trees out front, a little garden in the back, and a small lake to sit in front of in the evening.

"Well Paul I guess we could be here for a long time, if we even keep time anymore."

"Yes dear, I think it's lovely and you did a great job in picking it out."

"We did it together."

Paul kissed her and picked her up and carried her across the threshold. After all in this world they have the body of a 25 year old.

This morning they were able to sleep in real late, because it was Wednesday, and Brenda had a class at nine a.m. So she would not wake them and she didn't know how long they slept. Paul rolled over and said in a very soft sweet voice "dear its 12:34 pm, we are just waking up, and I love being a Wayshower!"

"I love you, you silly man."

"Okay enough of that, I'm starving and I don't think we even ate in our other world last night."

"No we didn't, let's have some cereal and then we'll work on brunch."

"Yes and no, let's have cereal and then let's go to Brenda's school and take her out to lunch." Margo liked that idea even better.

"I'm going to do some writing. See you in an hour." Margo

then took her pad out to the lake, sat her tea down on the table in the gazebo, and wrote this.

Next Dimension

A new Earth it will be,
wonderful for you and me.

All our wishes are for the taken,
open your Heart and start making.

Here we help each other without a thought,
the food here is delicious, and can't be bought.

Play or build, whatever you inspire,
and with nothing to impede your desire.

Swim with the dolphins in the sea,
or you could fly around, just like a bee.

Margo Brown Miller 2028

The World Government is celebrating fifteen years of world peace, and an all-time low for hunger. Also the new army of peace has obtained full levels of tolerance for all peoples, regardless of age, color, religion or sexual preference. As long as you are a peaceful person, you are free to live in this world by your own means. Source unknown

Their dreams were becoming more frequent and up to four nights a week.

Margo walked into the den carrying some hot tea and scones for her and Paul. "Dear I brought you something."

He was reading a science journal about cell testing of new

synthetic bodies for humans. He put the papers down and said "my dear sweet Margo, come to visit me have you?"

She smiled and said "yes I would like to talk with you about our dreams."

"Okay then let's talk."

"Well, we have been really doing a lot of work in the new Earth and it's great. My question is when are we going to start getting our stuff here in order? I'm mostly talking legal stuff."

"That's a good question dear, we could be gone any time now, let's sit down with the girls, and discuss it."

Margo was starting to get confused between the two worlds. She and Paul were just not up to taking care of the farm the way it needed to be anymore. Brenda was helping anyway she could, but with school and all it was a bit much. It just so happens that Terames had been advising Tamla and Shasha that it was time to leave D.C. and come back home to Alabama. This night knowledge would be given.

"Paul we are at the High Council tonight."

"Yes we are dear maybe we'll see the girls."

Ringo motioned them to come over to where he was and they did.

Then Paul said "hey everyone is here tonight."

Terames said "yes we are, and we are going to talk about getting things in order."

"Mom we were just talking about that, two days ago."

She smiled and said "I know."

This was the first big family reunion they've had in a while. Paul and Margo's parents were there, Jenny and Cory Greene were there, and Tamla, Shasha, and Brenda were there of course. The most important one there was the Honorable Ambrosia and

Ambrosia had this all planned out.

Margo said "it is so good to have you here Your Grace, thank you for residing over our adventures."

"Margo you honor me always, especially with your poems."

There was no arguing over who gets this or that it was mostly just time spent reminiscing with each other. Paul Sr. and Connor talked about their future in the new Earth and not the Korean War that was long gone from their memories.

Here is what Ambrosia imparted to Paul and Margo. "Tamla and Shasha are moving back to Alabama soon to live with you and Brenda, Cory and Jenny will join you in your dreams on the new Earth occasionally, to start preparing for their time to come, and you will sign everything over to Tamla and Shasha so they will attend to you during your time on Earth. Then lastly you two are going to spend more and more time on the new Earth functioning there."

They both told Ambrosia that these are the first things they are going to work on in the morning. One thing you can count on is the sun was out and they were both wide awake.

This knowledge that was given to them was very helpful and they were a little confused before talking with Ambrosia. They were tired and forgetful in this world, but in the new Earth they were more alive and sharp as a tack.

It was Saturday so Brenda was with them for breakfast. Paul was coming back with some fresh eggs and the girls were making pancakes.

Margo put her arm around Brenda and said "did you know you are a God send?"

"Grandma when I first saw you I knew you were my

grandma."

"Well dear you are certainly ours."

Paul walked in and said "plenty of eggs today, think I'll make some egg salad later."

They both looked at each other and pretended to scream. "Ha real funny, I'm an excellent cook!" he said.

Paul was in the den after breakfast getting ready to write a letter to the science journal, that he was reading about cell research, and DNA to create these synthetic bodies in. As he started to dictate his letter he then thought *I should ask Ringo or better yet Amerorth first before I publish this.*

Margo had woken from a nap and Brenda was reading so Margo wrote this.

Many Hearts

Family is certainly not just blood,
when one of us bleeds there is a flood.

The secret is to treat your friends well,
therefore in doing so, a true family will dwell.

You've done your part to say,
I Love these people in every way.

Receive all that is given to you,
and give all that your Heart tells you to.

This will make you stand tall,
not in an ego way that will fall.

When we acknowledge that we are one,
then our time on this Earth will be done.

This is not easy to acquire,
to be tried in the Sun's fire.

I have nothing else to impart,
but to be free, and follow your Heart.

Margo Brown Miller 2029

CHAPTER 20

Twenty-eight years and she was ready to retire and return home. Their little girl was now on her way to becoming a Heart Surgeon and they couldn't be more proud. Tamla was finishing up her business with the staff and preparing the next candidate to replace her. Her new replacement had been working on her staff for several years as one of her speech writers. He hails from a little town near Montgomery and graduated from Auburn with a B. A. in Political Science and his law degree from George Mason.

Before Tamla left she wrote this for the records.

I've seen many things in this life and the one to come. My parents are part of the avant-garde of Wayshowers that came here many years ago. And I know in my Heart that they will leave this present Earth soon. Now it could be termed unfair to know where they are going and It's even more unfair to have travelled there with them in many dreams, but this is part of the large plan from above. Some even call it heaven, and this I know that the new Earth is heavenly. My mom has served her country and state and I just pray that I've followed in her footsteps the best I could. People are different this is nature, and to try and control them will hurt the soul. To believe that God hates this or calls that sin is not the way we should believe. For if God is Love then where do we find a place to stand in judgement of others? This is where government should and sometimes does step in, for its very existence comes from the collective of us all. I won't say I've fought for this or that, but I will say it's been an honor to carry the fight for the people's rights. Thank you.

Honorable Congresswoman Tamla Miller-Greene 2029

They were on their way back home to Montgomery when their new reverse gravity car took them on a detour. Without getting too futuristically technical, let's just say it broke down, and they were somewhere around Richmond, Virginia. These   two were so young when they moved to Washington, D. C. to work on Margo's staff and during that time they fell in love. Now over thirty-five years of living in Washington D.C. they were concerned if they would like going back to live in Alabama.

Shasha called the insurance company to fix the car and said to Tamla "well dear I guess we might as well stay the night here, since we got a late start anyway."

Tamla looked around and said "sure once we get the car taken care of and on it's way to the shop then we'll find a place."

It's strange that they spent many dinners on the Potomac with each other and yet tonight was even more special.

Tamla said "my dear you did a great job finding this French cuisine."

Shasha picked up her wine glass and said "a toast, to my best friend all these years and now we embark on another journey together. I love you Tamla my friend and partner."

Tamla moved her glass to Shasha's and then said "same to you we do make a great team."

This night their dreams will take them somewhere special again. Tamla said as she looked around "Grandma we are on the new Earth are we not going to the Council?"

"No dear you and Shasha will be coming here once a week to help out."

Shasha said "that's going to be fun grandma."

"Yes but I won't be your Guide anymore. Margo will help you both when you come here. Paul will become Brenda's Guide and help her with being a doctor."

Tamla said "grandma what are you going to do?"

"I am to become the assistant to the High Councilor Ambrosia."

Two days later and they are on the farm and ready to help. Jenny and Cory were there to welcome them also. Paul could not move around like he used too and Margo just walked over to give them a hug.

Cory said "girls let me help you with your bags."

Paul yelled at Cory with a laugh and said "young whipper snapper showing off."

Cory and Jenny laughed and she said "Paul we love you too."

So now the house has Paul, Margo, Tamla, Shasha and Brenda, Cory and Jenny live not too far away.

They had become more and more comfortable in the new Earth. Paul would say to Margo "I'm ready to go to sleep and return to our new home."

Brenda understood but didn't know how she would act when that will happen for good. She would tell him "grandpa you will be on the new Earth, but you will then be my Guide, and I will be with you once a week."

He smiled and said "yes my young apprentice and I will be your master."

Margo laughed and said "you will always be a silly man."

The dinner table was something to behold, fresh fruits and vegetables with some delicious pasta with white creamy basil topped with a Gouda cheese sauce and a very fine wine from the Hood River region in Oregon. The best thing Shasha learned while living in Georgetown was how to cook fine cuisine.

Margo said "Shasha you are an excellent cook, you should have your own restaurant."

A wonderful dinner and a fine wine made for a very comfortable night for sleep, and tonight the whole family were together in dreamland this night. Shasha said "mom, dad you two are here with us that's great." She then walked over and gave them a big hug.

They smiled at her and mom said "yes dear we're starting our process of coming here more often."

Paul and Margo walked over and Margo asked Ringo "what are we doing tonight?"

He replied "like I said before, you're on your own to explore this new Earth."

Brenda said "let's go to grandma and grandpa's home and make some lunch." They all thought of how wonderful the food tasted there and agreed to her suggestion.

The night was spent together where they even had time to go swim in the oceans and then fly through the air, then over, and under the water a time or two. Tamla said to Shasha "remember when we were young and we first swam with these dolphins?"

"My dear I do remember how wonderful that was and is every time we do."

Cory said "I remember how I fell in love with Jenny that night and how special it was, oh what a night."

Paul and Margo didn't wake-up, that's what Brenda thought. She knocked on their door and no answer. It was 1:11 pm and they still weren't up. She walked downstairs and said to her moms "grandma and grandpa aren't waking up." They both looked at the clock and stood up and rushed upstairs to find Paul in the hallway.

"What's up" he said.

Tamla laughed and said "you are I see, where's mom?"

He smiled and said "in the bathroom of course."

Margo coming out said "family I am taking my notebook and walking out to the gazebo to write."

A beautiful Alabama afternoon, the sun was shining bright, and the birds were singing. The fragrance of her flowers filled the air and looking at the reflection from the lake said it all. She knew that this was her last day in this body. She had a lot to reflect on, but could only hold her thoughts long enough to write this.

God is Love

To continue in this form seems unreal,
my Spirit knows what to think and how to feel.

A life here of so many good years,
only brings my Heart to cry many happy tears.

I'll never forget where I'm from,
now knowledgeable of what is to come.

For in the new Earth I have a home,
Where my Spirit is so very free to roam.

Worlds are everywhere for this we know,
a part of our creation in that we will grow.

Continue to hold Love very dear,
it's our number one weapon against fear.

I Am, is the name Moses was told,
together we are God, and precious as gold.

The Master Jesus said "I Am the way",
god is Love and there is nothing else to say.

Margo Brown Miller 2032

CHAPTER 21

Now that everyone in their family group has woke up, only Margo and Paul still remained on the new Earth. Margo looked around and said to Paul "well dear looks like we aren't going back."

"I guess we've made the transition dear."

They spent the rest of the day reflecting on their last day on the old Earth, and preparing for their first full day on the new one. Now it is true that they're in a different state of being, where rest, food, and the other things that are required in the third dimensional self are not as important now. They would go to sleep to visit the other Earth or other worlds. Paul and Margo were thinking about their old home on the farm, and how the family was, now that they are gone.

When Brenda headed upstairs to wake up her grandparents, she was surprised. Knock, knock and she said "grandma, grandpa it's time to wake up." She then looks at the clock in the hall and notices the time is 1:11. Two more knocks and still no answer, she then opens the door, and walking in to the bed she touches her grandma. She tells her "time to wake up." No response! Her heart skips a beat and she holds her breath. With no response from both of them, a tear begins to fall down her cheek then quietly she turns around, and goes downstairs crying.

It's strange that even with this advanced knowledge of eternity, she would still miss them. I guess it has to do with using a whole new way of communication?

Shasha was in the kitchen when Tamla looked up the stairs to see Brenda crying. She went to her and opened her arms for knew what had happened. She said "my dear sweet baby, everything will be fine."

"I know mom, but it is still different." A big hug from mom and they both went downstairs to tell Shasha.

Brenda walks toward Shasha and opens her arms "mom, we need to contact emergency services for grandma and grandpa. They are no longer with us."

Shasha's eyes got big and she said "you mean they have left us?"

"Yes mom, they have." All the while Tamla made the contact and the authorities were on their way. The girls just sat together in the den and cried and consoled one another.

Paul and Margo were there watching as the whole thing transpired. Paul opened his arms, hugged Margo, and said "dear this is all part of the plan."

"I know it is, it just breaks my heart to see my girls cry and not be able to say or do anything."

"I know my sweet, but we will talk with them this Friday

night." That seemed to put a smile on her face.

In their will they made sure not to indicate how they wanted their remains disposed of. Tamla contacted Governor Newberry of the state of Alabama, where she made sure that the Honorable Congresswoman, and former Governor Margret Brown Miller would have a proper burial. The governor made sure that they would have Dr. Paul Miller with her also.

The lines were long, even the President of the World was there to hear former Congresswoman Tamla Miller-Greene speak eloquently of her mother, but it was Governor Newberry that did it best when she said.

"I will dispense with the titles for this most powerfully kind human that graced us. Margo spent her lifetime helping others, and loving all to make this planet a friendlier place to live. When I ran against her many years ago, I knew I wouldn't win, but I knew that being around her and watching what she did would be important to me. I couldn't have been more correct on knowing that she would and did do that. So, I will close with asking her to continue to guide us and shine her Light for our path forward. We love and miss you Margret Brown Miller."

There were kind words said about Dr. Paul Miller from his friends that were still around. They had many great things to say about him. Brenda said something very touching to all about her grandpa. She talked about how he was so excited to find out that she wanted to be a medical doctor like him. She couldn't say enough about how much she loved and respected him and will continue to communicate with him.

It's a good thing that they had been coming here for several years to their new home. The funny thing about it was that the Avant-garde had a big hand in setting this new Earth into being.

Margo was ready to start governing in a very special way. This first day in their new surroundings would be filled with much hope. Paul would be spending his time with the other scientific people studying what had been accomplished in the last Earth age.

The new government would take advantage of all that was learned on Earth before. Here Margo was a chief just like her mom, and she would continue to train Tamla to be one as well. Today was the day that the Wayshowers started their new lives here. This day the High Councilor Ambrosia would preside over the Assembly. She was so excited when she saw her mom there, and said "mom, it's so good to see you here again, especially on this special day."

"Dear I wouldn't miss this for any world."

With the assembly in its first session, one of the chiefs said "I make a motion to create a constitution for this new government." Margo and many others there were thinking this is *Deja vu*. Now almost all of the inhabitants there were part of some form of government on the old Earth. Margo joined in with many others to second the motion. After that they decided to form several groups to brain storm and come up with this new document.

The meeting was starting to become somewhat chaotic with all the groups discussing their ideas. That's when Terames addressed the Speaker of the day said "Madame Speaker I would like to make a motion for order in the House."

The Speaker looked at her and said "Assistant High Councilor Terames that would be my honor."

Then her gavel fell hard on the table and she said "order in the House."

The House became quiet and Terames said "the High Councilor Ambrosia would like to speak."

Ambrosia said "please be seated, I would like your attention. Today is a very, very special day for our kind. After over 25,000 years on the planet Earth, it is now time for the next stage in our galactic development to begin. I would encourage all of you to be very cognitive of what happened before. Remember how our people would slowly move toward being more civilized to the point of near perfection. Then things got easy and there were many wars because most of you forgot our mission. This is like I said, part of this development will be that you are held responsible to see that you govern in peace, and in love. After all we are taught that Love is the Way and that it does conquer all."

Margo thought about the words of Ambrosia so she decided to write to commemorate this day. It took some time to gather her thoughts, and wrote.

Laws of the Heart

Hope is eternal for so we shall say.
Using Love we create good laws this day.

We choose Love, for fear leads to hate.
Love shines the greater light for us to relate.

By guiding our Hearts we make shadows of the night.
We follow the light of Love for we know that's right.

Gather your thoughts on this to blend.
Join us with your Heart and then it will mend.

Today was the day for a picnic and that's all that was on Paul's mind. So when he and Margo had their breakfast he put the question to her "dear let's spend today together and have a picnic."

Margo looked at him rather puzzled and said "that is an excellent idea, where do you want to go?"

"Let's fly around until we see a spot that we like."   After saying that, off they went, flying around this new Earth. They went over some beautiful green mountains and through a blue vertical sea. While they were there they communicated with some dolphins and a blue whale.

Paul said "hello there blue whale, what's your name?"

The blue whale said "it's Charley, don't ask me where I got, but I believe some kids gave me the name."

Margo said "Charley is a great name and it suits you well."

"Thank you Margo."

Margo was surprised and said "how did you know my name?"

"We know all of your names and we have been waiting for you."

Paul just smiled and said "now that makes me feel very welcome, thank you Charley my new friend."

They spent some time with the mountain animals too, they even met a couple of squirrels, and befriended them. Paul spotted a little pond and said "Margo, how about down there?"

She looked and said "let's go." After they set up the picnic and ate, then it was time to reflect. Margo asked him "why did you want to do this?"

"I just felt like I did when we met at Woodstock. I wanted

to spend the day with you and share all my good feelings."

"That is so sweet and this day is marvelous."

The air was so clean and the birds were singing so beautifully that Paul said "we had so few days like this on the old Earth, but when we did they were so memorable, and I believe those feelings were stored inside for this present time together. I mean look at us, we look and feel like we did when we were in our 20's. This is such an opportunity to rekindle some of those old experiences again, but this time we consciously live them."

Young Again

Remembering that we were young once before.
Was all we wanted and it was everything to adore.

Then in time we would gain knowledge with age.
Only to learn from a Master, who would be our sage

(Chorus)
Live your life and Love, pure and as white as a dove.
Don't judge what you see, let it live and let it be.

The day will come to you,
when your youth will be returned,
and your life is all brand new.

So go and gather all,
you've been given the call.

Paul read this and said "Margo my dear, now you're writing songs, and this one is wonderful."

"Why thank you, I wrote one in the Assembly yesterday too. I want to implement songs as part of our constitution and laws."

"Now that is an interesting idea, if things rhymed then we would remember them better."

"I've always thought if we had music to orchestrate our lives that maybe there would be harmony between us all."

"Now I like that because after all we are vibrations just like music. The sweeter the vibrations the sweeter the music would be."

After returning home Paul kissed Margo goodnight and said "you are now my new world."

CHAPTER 22

Since they don't really track time on the new Earth, it would seem that there would be some means of determining when things are to happen.

If you're not sure where this is heading then let me explain. Paul is Brenda's guide, Margo has taken over to be Tamla and Shasha's guide, so how do Paul, and Margo know when they will be visited by them? I'll tell you, they let the universe guide them and tonight it decided to have some visitors from Earth.

Paul was so happy to see his granddaughter again. He said to her "Dr. Brenda Miller-Greene MD, how are you doing my dear?"

"Doing very well grandpa, how are you, and grandma?"

"We are fine and still so very proud of you. I've been following your progress at the Heart center and I see that you are coming up with some very special theories to correct the causes of heart failures."

"Thanks, I owe a lot of it to your teaching me in the Spiritual arts."

He then moved over to her and said "give me a big hug" and Brenda did so happily.

Margo explained to Tamla how they were attempting to run their new government with songs.

"So mom how does that work?"

"Well dear you first need to have your people on the same frequency or at least within a certain bandwidth."

"Okay mom what would be your suggestions for that on this present Earth?"

"I would find a reason to galvanize your people under a common goal. Now do not use fear as a tool because it will only lead to madness."

"Hum, I'll have to study on that one with Shasha more."

Shasha was so excited because tonight not only was she visited by the Miller's, but her parents where there too, and Cory asked her "what do you want to do tonight?"

"I would like to have a big family reunion now that Paul and Margo have both made the transition."

"I see your point, especially since your mom and I are following right behind them, and I'm sure we will have a lot to learn from them as they are the avant-garde."

Jenny just stood there and enjoyed listening to her two favorite people make plans for the evening.

Later that evening (or day in their dreams), the family were there all together at the Miller home. This would be nothing new they used to have these little reunions a few times a month on the Earth.

Paul waited until everyone was seated at the table when he made his speech.

"Family we are gathered here today (or tonight in your dreams) to officially celebrate our transition to the new Earth. We are now part of this new Earth and no longer reside in the three dimensional reality of the old one. Not to bore you with too much of the meta-physics of this, I will just say that we are now in a fourth dimensional reality which doesn't use time in the same way as before. Hopefully today many of your questions will start to be answered."

Their conversations started flowing in all directions, then Margo stood up, and said "family, we have only been here a week in your time and we too have many questions. So, let's enjoy our meal, and then we can start."

The rest of the meal was spent enjoying the food and the company they were having together, and this time Conner, Paul Sr. and Lucille were there too.

In their home was a big conference type room that they had planned for meetings just like this. This room had been in their dreams for many years. Margo opened up the conversation with "we have been told that this new Earth is our opportunity to improve on the things we learned on the former Earth."

Jenny asked her "will we perform our current professions in this new Earth or will we receive new ones?"

"That's a very good question and I can only answer it this way for now. Hopefully more insight will be given as we live here. So here's a short song for you Jenny, my friend."

Heart Preparations

Now, before you come here for good,
I strongly suggest that you would.

Do the things your Heart tells you to,
then live your life just the way you do.

Give your free time to your Hearts call,
on that day you will be able to stand tall.

Paul then said "I couldn't agree more."

The family started to decide what they were going to do for the rest of the visit. Then Terames and Ringo arrived and Tamla shouted "Grandma!"

"Why hello granddaughter I see we have the whole family here tonight."

"Yes we do, we were just about to make decisions for our visit."

"Okay dear, Ringo and I need to split you up for some important learning. Margo, we will need you, Paul, Paul Sr., Connor, and Lucille to perform these."

Being the natural organizer Margo read the teaching assignments from the board "Paul and Paul Sr. with Brenda, I will be with Tamla and Shasha, Connor with Cory, Lucille with Jenny. That's the list of what is planned."

Paul Sr. said "I like this list, both Paul and I, couldn't be more excited than to teach our Brenda all that we know. She is an exceptionally gifted and a Heart centered person."

"Yes she is so inquisitive that she will keep you both busy." Margo said and then went to talk with Tamla and Shasha.

Margo thoughts were, *this new Earth is looking more, and more promising each day.* Then she told Paul "Dear, I'm going to work in the Assembly today."

"What's going on in there today?"

"We are starting the process of finalizing our new Constitution."

"Good luck honey, I think it took our fore fathers some eleven years to get the first one done."

She just looked at him and said "men."

"You are so right, we really suffered not having women involved all those years, and you've done your gender proud."

She walked over to him and grabbed his head and kissed him.

Today's session holds so much promise and the people of the new Earth are eager to start. Margo took her seat, then looked around, but she didn't see Ambrosia. She asked Terames "mom, have you seen Ambrosia?"

"She's not going to attend today dear."

"Oh okay, guess we're on our own then."

Terames smiled and said "well, I guess I'm just chopped liver then?"

Margo laughed and said "sorry mom."

Some time went by and the Speaker rapped the gavel down and said "order, order let's bring this Assembly to order. Okay let's begin with the business of the day." The room was quiet and the Speaker said "when we left last time we agreed to come back with some new ideas for our Constitution, so let's start."

Most of the ideas were based on the final World

Constitution that is still in effect in the third dimensional Earth today. However this is the fourth dimension and things are a little different here.

When it was Chief Margo's turn she offered this.

The Law of Love

Believe in Love now it's our moment to,
because this will be shown in all that we do.

So we should never stray from this creed,
therefore we can show the Light of Love indeed.

We can create a new Earth from the start.
As we treat each other as ourselves.
Let us help one another from our Heart.

While we travel into this fourth dimension here,
where together we form the new way that is clear.

In the doing of our jobs will be our binding,
to treasure our new lives in all we are finding.

A world not controlled by fear or desire.
This is our new hope of Love and Peace.
In our world we achieve goals much higher.

The whole Assembly sat there quiet until she sat down. Then one stood and clapped, joined by many more, until the whole house was up applauding. Margo stood and with tears rolling down her face, just smiled, and waved. Terames held her hand and then lifted it up. The Speaker let this go for a while, then rapped the gavel, and said "Chief Margo, that was beautiful" as he was holding back tears.

The rest of the meeting went very well. Margo was able to convince them that the new Constitution should at least rhyme. She was happy to get that done.

Meanwhile Paul was working with Ringo on some frequency vibration tests. He was going over some books from Atlantis on the subject. Then to his surprise Amerorth showed up.

Paul said "my friend, it's been a long time. How are you doing?"

"Just fine Paul, still teaching up on the moon base."

"I know I miss that place."

"Well maybe you can go there and help me teach."

"That would be awesome."

Ringo just listened and said "well now that we're all caught up let's go over these tests shall we?"

Amerorth asked them "what are you guys working on?"

Paul looked at Ringo and then answered "well we are testing some healing for our bone structures by using certain frequencies of vibrations. This will be of little use here, but on the third dimension it could help a lot of people."

"How are you going to get this information to Earth?"

Ringo said "we will need to plant it in the mind of a doctor of Osteopathic Medicine."

"Right we can use Brenda to make the suggestion to one of her colleagues."

Amerorth then said "you've got a good plan there and maybe Brenda will meet another Indigo?"

Paul invited Amerorth to return home with him and Ringo for dinner. On their arrival Paul greeted Margo with a kiss and then said "look, my friend Amerorth is back!"

She just chuckled and said "I am so happy that he is back.

Amerorth, he did miss you and the moon base just as well."

Paul then said "I'm sorry dear, how was your day at the Assembly?"

"Well my motion passed to create laws that will rhyme."

All three men clapped and Paul said "dear with you helping to run things, then we are in good hands."

CHAPTER 23

A great division was beginning on the old Earth with the people starting to choose sides of how they should live. This was a problem in areas of medicine because the establishment was becoming more and more progressive, but some in authority couldn't seem to grasp the changes that were happening.

With more people making the transition to the new Earth, the fearful in power were giving them mind altering drugs. This was being done because what was happening to them was not understood and by drugging these people they were in a sense robbing their selves of the knowledge that could be given to assist in the changes to come.

Dr. Brenda Miller-Greene was trying her best to prevent this knowledge from being destroyed. At a meeting of the effects that stress and loneliness have on the heart, she included some of this in her speech. She had listened to her colleagues and applauded one of them who mentioned how important the heart was for our day to day decisions. When it was her turn to speak this is what she said.

"My fellow colleagues and honored guests. I would like to take this opportunity to address a subject that is very interrelated to the function of the heart. We need to make some in the medical community aware of how much more electrical energy the heart creates compared to the brain and the using of mind altering drugs for people that are becoming older is causing them not to remember things as well as when they were younger. All this is doing is hurrying them in becoming inert while they are still alive. How about we give them a healthy diet and let them just finish their days here in dignity? I feel they have so much left to offer and who knows maybe they can share some of the next phase of their incarnation with us? Let's support the heart in any way we can and protecting the rest of the body this will do just that. Thank you all very much."

As she sat down, the applause was thunderously loud. Now Paul and Paul Sr. weren't there officially, but they sure were in Spirit, and they watched the whole thing. Of course Cory and Jenny were in the audience with Tamla, and Shasha, so she sat right there next to them.

Cory said "granddaughter you make us so proud, that was beautiful."

"Thanks granddad, I have learned so much about love from you all."

Jenny said "dear, you know grandpa Paul was there too."

She just smiled and looked at her moms just sitting there taking it all in.

Brenda went up to her room to get some notes that she had written down. As she returned Shasha asked "sweetie, what do you have there?"

"Just some notes about the heart, I've been jotting down. I plan on asking Grandpa Paul some questions Friday in our dreams. I thought if I studied them I might have a better chance of remembering."

Tamla and Shasha both laughed, and agreed how they hoped it works.

Shasha said "sweetie your mom and I have been trying that and sometimes it seems to help."

Then Tamla said "always worth a try, we always have questions for mom, grandma and Ambrosia when we visit."

Jenny said "Cory and I are currently working on our transition and we have a lot of questions, but we figure we need to learn to just live in it."

Brenda then said "I'm not in a hurry for you two to leave yet. I'm still dealing with the other grandparents that have already done that."

Cory said "we understand, we aren't ready yet either, but it's nice to know where we are going."

"Well granddad, I look forward to our weekly visits with them on the new Earth, especially grandpa Paul."

Tamla and Shasha came over to them, and Shasha said "we need a big group hug."

Dr. Brenda Miller-Greene continues to help the elderly with more natural medical treatments and lots of love.

As they were enjoying breakfast a small issue arose. Paul asked Margo "dear when you are at the Assembly, what if anything, do the people there call this new Earth?"

"That is a very good question and I can't recall anyone addressing the name of this new Earth."

"Well, I'm getting tongue tied when the family visits and I have to say old Earth or new Earth. It just seems that maybe we should decide if this is a new Earth or a new planet?"

"Okay, I will bring that up in the Assembly today."

While working with some the other doctors and scientists they started discussing the life expectancy of their current bodies.

Paul said to the group "fellow colleagues, we should determine the life span of these bodies. Any suggestions on how we do that?"

One of the scientist said "we can run some DNA tests to gain more knowledge about them."

Another one said "or we can ask our guides."

Then another doctor said "I tried to ask questions about the planet and I was told that we need to continue to discover things because this is still part of our advancement."

Paul was satisfied and announced "we will begin our studies in a way to obtain a starting point of who we are at this present time."

When one of his colleagues said "we should get the test data that had been gathered from the old Earth."

Paul couldn't help but use this opportunity to say "great idea" and then say "I have another question it's small but I feel very important."

One scientist said "okay doctor, what is your question?"

"Thanks, I would like for us to consider what we should call this planet we are on. What I mean is this, is this a new Earth or another planet?" They deliberated until lunch.

Returning from lunch the group seemed to have a new name for their planet. "Dr. Miller, we believe that a name has been chosen and we are all in agreement. Would you like for me to announce the name?"

"Yes please Dr. Newton."

"Being that this planet is so green and blue. The wildlife is so friendly and we can communicate with them. The temperature is always pleasant and the vegetation perfectly tends to our needs."

"Okay Dr. Newton, is the name Eden then?"

"No Dr. Miller, its name is Atlantis!"

Paul thought for a moment and said "I like it!"

During this time, Margo was in her group in the Assembly, and working on some new laws.

"Margo, I believe that we need to keep our new laws simple, but we should still make sure everyone is protected."

"I agree Bill, even though things are peaceful and all the people respect each other. There could be a time when people start to forget the past and start treating each other badly."

Janet then chimed in and said "I agree with you both, but we certainly don't want to force this on anyone. I've always felt that we get along better when we choose to do this together."

The group was in agreement all they they just needed was to come up with the proper law. Hopefully this would never be an issue now or in the future.

They broke for lunch and Margo wished to be alone with her thoughts. During the break her thoughts where about her time on the old Earth in politics and she put them into a song.

After returning Margo made a motion "I would like to present this song to the Assembly."

Achievement

Many things I learned in my last life,
of an imperfect world filled with strife.

A future in hope this I knew,
to love all the people, not just a few.

Some were good and a few even bad,
but knowing all along not to become sad.

To govern the best way I could,
always striving to do what was good.

Our new home should have a name,
then rekindle the good from the same.

Know that our way is to be true,
always to keep in our Spirits view.

Atlantis, true and new
Atlantis, green and blue
Atlantis, we love you

The entire Assembly was in agreement that this song should be entered into the record. The Speaker then made a motion to ask Margo a question.

"Yes, Mr. Speaker, what is your question?"

"Mrs. Miller, I would like to ask why you slipped in that part about naming the planet Atlantis."

"Mr. Speaker, my husband and I were talking about that this morning and how confusing it is to refer to our new planet as the new Earth, and then the former as the old Earth."

The Assembly then took a vote and agreed to call their

new planet Atlantis.

Later that day, Margo and Paul were home sharing their day. "Paul I have something exciting to tell you."

Even though he was just as excited to tell her his news, he still said "go ahead dear, I will tell you my news next."

"Okay, I asked the members of the Assembly if we could name this planet something other than the new Earth and we all agreed to name it..."

Paul then interrupted and said "Atlantis!"

"Yes, how did you know?"

"Well we did the same thing today."

"Wow, I guess it was meant to be." They so wanted to be together alone tonight that they asked their guides not to disturb them.

Our True Essence

Living your life in Love is so fine.
To be measured and remembered.
For each day is a good time.

Another dimension can't explain.
How it would feel any different.
When loved on any dimensional plane.
The Heart has all the power.
Let it be your guide to bring.
It's Love to you in any hour.

If Love is not near the Heart will melt.
Life's not wonderful when it's away.
Love closer to the Heart to be felt.

I'm in Love as much as before.
I won't ever harden my Heart.
Or want to close its door.

Love is not a thing.
Love for you to bring.
Love is doing your part.
Love lives in your heart.

CHAPTER 24

More and more Wayshowers have been coming in to Atlantis. The number is very close to the 144,000 that volunteered to come to Earth. When this number is complete they have been told that the remaining Souls from Earth will start coming to Atlantis shortly after that happens.

Margo was at the Assembly when Terames said "dear it's time to finalize the new Constitution and have the government in place before the people start arriving."

"I know mom, when is Ambrosia going to come back to our Assembly?"

"She will stop by soon, she has been working in another solar system."

"Wow, we are spread out that much?"

"Dear, you still have a way to go in your development, and we all do."

Paul was there with Ringo and he noticed Cory was there too. "Cory, how are you doing and where is Jenny?"

"Well, she's not visiting tonight but, she will visit on Friday with the rest of the family."

"Okay, so why are you here without her?"

"My friend, I've crossed over."

Paul was numb and he didn't know what to say. He thought about Jenny being without him and then said "I guess you will be looking for... Connor, I see you are here to greet Cory!"

Margo ran over to see her daddy. "Daddy, how have you been? Sorry we haven't contacted you sooner, but I've been busy working with mom, and getting this new government set up."

"I know dear, me and a lot of Vets have been preparing some documents to present to the Assembly about how to avoid any future wars."

"That sounds great daddy, I want to read them when you are done."

"Okay, we'll have them completed soon."

The Assembly was about to begin with the business of the day. Then the Assistant High Councilor Terames said "Ms. Speaker, I would like to address the Assembly."

"Yes, Your Grace you may have the floor."

"Thank you Ms. Speaker. Atlantians, I need to give you some more knowledge for your current growth. As you know your fellow Wayshowers are leaving the third dimensional plane, they will be transitioning to this planet and into the fourth dimension soon. Even though time is not the same here, we still need to prepare for when that number is reached, because that's when the rest of the Souls from Earth will start coming. So I would encourage you to get this Constitution written down ASAP. Thank you." That's when Margo presented her plan.

The Bridge

Set your Heart for the intention of the Soul.
Follow the Light and hold its energy.
Use this knowledge to understand your goal.

Visualize the picture from your Heart.
Energy will form in this sphere.
Stimulation will grow and begin to start.

All power is projected in a ray.
Soul and ego will dissolve.
Spirit is now ready for the Way.

Pray to the Great Spirit of life.
Listen for the Spirit to move.
Release from the present strife.

Stabilization of this Bridge is growing.
That connects the Spirit to the Source.
Bringing the Light its Love flowing.

Resurrect the Spirit from its fall.
Become one through ascension.
The Source is from us and for all.

After she sat down, there was nothing but silence, and you could have heard a pin drop. They didn't know whether to applaud or just sit and think on her words.

Then the assistant High Councilor Terames said "Ms. Speaker, may I address this Assembly?"

"Yes Your Grace, you may do so."

"Thank you, Atlantians I do believe these words should conclude, your first Constitution of this planet Atlantis."

One after another announced motions to make it so, and with a voice vote this concluded the first Constitution of Atlantis.

Paul and Margo went home, but before that they invited Connor, and Cory to join them. Terames and Ringo needed to return to the Pleiades. The four of them spent the next couple of days discussing their new government, and getting current information from Cory about the daily activity of Earth.

Jenny laid there in bed noticing the sunlight beaming in, *but why is he not awake* she thought? As she lay there breathing very shallow, she wondered why Cory wasn't awake. A chill went down her spine, when she knew that he had made the transition in the night. Gently she said "Cory dear are you awake?" There were many tears shed for this man that she loved so much that day.

The Greene's had moved in with the girls some years ago and this morning Jenny would tell them. She quietly got out of bed, went to the door and started downstairs. Shasha noticed her walking down the stairs and she said "mom, where's dad?"

"He's no longer with us dear."

She walked over there, put her arms around her mom, and said "I love you mom."

"I love you too dear and I'm going to miss him."

Brenda and Tamla were making breakfast when they sat down at the table. Brenda turned around and noticed they were crying and she said "what's wrong, where's granddad, oh, no!"

Tamla was there to hold her baby girl. "Your granddad is with my mom and dad. We'll see him in two more nights."

"I know mom, I knew this would happen, I just didn't want it to."

That evening Jenny called on her guide Lucille before turning in. She asked about Cory's transition and was it his choice or just his time. Lucille answered all her questions, then said that he didn't want to leave her, but he understood that it was his time. She awoke the next morning with a renewed sense of life, knowing that she was with the people she loved, and that she would be with Cory tomorrow night.

Paul put his arm around Cory's shoulder and said "you know those women will be fine."

"You know that's right" that was one of Cory's favorite things to say. He and Paul spent the rest of the day together just exploring Atlantis. Margo spent the day with her mom and mother-law Lucille.

Knowing it was only a dream didn't seem to matter to Jenny because she really wanted to be held by her man.

"Hello dear, did you miss me?" He said jokingly.

"Yes I did you left me in the middle of the night without even a warning."

"You know when I got here the first thing Paul asked me was where you were. It was then that I realized that I made the transition."

She then motioned to him to come to her and she said "you better hold me Cory Greene."

"Yes dear" he held her oh so tight.

The whole family was there and Brenda was next in line to hug granddad. "Granddad let's spend this time swimming with the dolphins."

Cory said "that's a great idea."

Then Paul said "hey I need to introduce you to my new friend Charley."

Brenda smiled and said "Charley, is he a tuna?"

"No he's a whale, silly."

Cory just laughed and said "this sounds like too much fun."

So they took off in flight swimming in and out, over and under any body of water they could find. They found some majestic waterfalls and decided to take a break there for lunch. The beauty was indescribable. Thinking of her friend Jenny, Margo wrote.

Jenny

Up this morning to greet the day.
No hugs or kisses will she feel.
For now her love has gone away.

He left during the night without a sound,
gone to another world, one that she knew,
and strong with courage that she has found.

She wants to be with him so much.
Dreaming of him will not do.
His Love for her is in his touch.

Oh my friend our Love is for you.
So you will be with your true Love.
That day your Heart will be new.

That day will come to you.
Your heart won't be blue.
That day will come to you.
Your Love is always true.

As the people on Atlantis were living with their new government there were some minor problems.

"Order, order we will have order in this house" said the Speaker pro tem.

"Thank you Mr. Speaker. I would like to address this body?"

"Please continue Mr. Jones."

"It has come to our attention that with the final Wayshowers arriving here daily, that we will need to implement an economic plan."

"Do you have one that you would like to offer?"

"No Mr. Speaker just a few thoughts I've put together."

"Okay then I put forward a motion before this house that we put a team together to work on this. All in favour say I, all opposed say no, sounds like the "I's" have it. The Speaker deems that this motion will go forward."

The teams were formed and Margo shared her plan with them. Her plan is to take the proposal and put it into a song or two.

Some of their long luncheon conversations went like this; "Okay Mr. Jones what are your ideas?" asked an Elder from the Taygete region. This region wasn't on Atlantis it was their region from the Pleiades. They didn't want to lose that part of their history.

"My thoughts are this; we don't need to work as we did before coming here, most of everything is provided through our thoughts, so do we need an economy or just something to do?"

Another elder said "This is so true, from what I gather we don't really age, if we do it's not very fast, and we all seem to be around 25. I'm positive that we don't procreate here either."

Mr. Jones then said "good work let's take our notes home and meet back here in a week."

Back at home Margo thought on this and said to Paul "dear we were talking in the assembly today about whether we need an economic system or not. What do you think about that?"

"Well we are in the process of studying data from earth on the human body. We are trying to determine how long these bodies will hold up. So I guess we need some scientific knowledge to go forward with that question."

"You are so right we need to gather information to make that call."

Later that evening Margo made this request in her dreams. "Mom, I have some questions to ask you and I would like a meeting with Ambrosia too."

"Well dear, let's start with your questions."

"Today in the Assembly, we formed teams to research whether or not we need to create an economy here on Atlantis. I would think that depending on how many souls will come, we might need to at least create some economic boundaries, and some type of currency?"

"This is true my daughter, the purpose here is to advance humanity further on this planet."

"Okay, but we haven't found a need for work, currencies or laws to govern us yet, and we are weary of the coming influx of people coming. We aren't sure of how many there might be." Margo then woke up and thought *I think mom helped me figure this out.*

She spent that morning jotting down notes of what they have in Atlantis to be grateful for. First thing food is plentiful, nourishing, and tastes divine. Second there is no need for fuel of any kind, because you can fly, food is fresh, and needs no cooking or cleaning. As she went along further with her list it dawned on her. *This seems so very similar to Eden, I wonder if...*

Atlantis

Hearts are full of Love and cheer.
We treat each other as ourselves.
Live free from any worry of fear.

Adam and Eve knew this feeling before.
Hearts are open and vibrate in Love.
Happy for this beautiful planet we adore.

Nothing is desired or to be hoped for.
So enjoy this time and create with Love.
That now we are here again once more.

Let's promise to live from the Heart.
Loving all creatures here as one family.
Always strive to live in Love is our part.

Live from the Heart
Always from the start
Live from the Heart
Just doing your part

The Assembly met again and discussed the business of whether they needed an economy or not. Margo listened to all of the group's ideas and by doing so she wrote their plan into a song.

Economy

Our hopes will rest, in doing what is best.
Treat each other as one, living under the Sun.
No need for justice to prevail, or an unneeded jail.

Live with no fear only Love, and only good we create.
Sharing all will sustain and Love will maintain.
To practice good for all, will keep us from a fall.

Keep no secrets hidden, or mistrust will be bidden.
Greed, envy and strife, will only cut like a knife.
Build the bridge to ascend, the next level to attend.

Honor all with Love, be as harmless as a dove.
Fear was used to correct, when Love was in neglect.
Love the world we're in, so we all will win.

This was a very big day for Atlantis, because the High Counsel sent all the chiefs, and Councilor Ambrosia was there too. At the end of the meeting when the document was signed by the Assembly, that's when Ambrosia put her signature to the document, and then searched for Margo to congratulate her for doing such a fine job. "Margo your idea to write the new Constitution into a series of songs was brilliant."

Terames was there too and so proud of her little girl that she said "dear you have done so well for the people here just like when you were on Earth. I'm sure being a Counselor is in your future."

"Thanks both of you I will first need to be an assistant High Councilor like you mom is."

CHAPTER 25

More Wayshowers were arriving and the group Margo had called "The Rebels" were now in Atlantis. The Assembly had made the announcement that all 144,000 Wayshowers were now accounted for and that the new Constitution had been signed. It's time to prepare because the Earth will start to release the remaining souls to Atlantis soon. Paul and Margo searched the database and located them.

With the Rebels located on Atlantis they planned for another get together and this will be the first one since 2012. Margo was anxious and called out to Paul "are we ready to go?"

"Yes we are, let's go get Cory and Jenny first."

Thinking about their get together with the rebels before on Earth caused Margo to say "This is so exciting, now we are all here permanently."

"I know I'm excited too and I think we need to start setting up some learning centers. This will allow us all to practice adjusting to living here as free and conscious beings."

"Well said Paul, maybe I should bring you to my Assembly meetings."

"What and not let me play in my lab, never!"

The team is now assembled and Margo is ready to address them. "My friends, my fellow southern US Wayshowers, it is my honor to have you back together, and here in our home." The whole group was so moved by her words that they stood and applauded.

Then Paul said "thank you all, she is still as wonderful as you remember her. Before we start discussing what our future plans are, I would like to start with any questions you may have."

Some in the group had just made the transition not too long ago and one of them was Joey Morgan. Who said "thank you Paul, I would like to know how long we will be here."

"Good question to start with Joey, we asked the High Counselor a lot of questions, and mostly we were told that we would need to discover them on our own. So to answer your question we have calculated around 1,000 years."

"Wow, that's a long time to live."

Katherine asked "is Atlantis another planet? If not why could we see it in the sky from Earth?"

"Well Atlantis is both, because she's the new Earth in the fourth dimension and our new home. The reason you could see her in the sky was because she's her own reflection."

Margo went over the new Constitution with them and she gave out copies to them all. Some of their questions were mostly like; what are they going to do during the time they are here. She didn't have all the answers and just like Paul she told them that Councilor Ambrosia had said they would need to discover them.

The rest of the afternoon was spent flying around, swimming with the dolphins, and Paul's friend Charley the blue whale.

What a wonderful day that was, Margo was excited, and couldn't wait to share this with the girls in her dream on Friday night. To understand that all this organizing would not be possible for Margo, and Paul, if they were still in their old bodies. Well that's not the case here on Atlantis, here the people are vibrant, caring, and friendly they have a heart for one another. They will work together to help all their fellow earthlings that are coming soon. But first it's Friday night, and the Miller's and Greene's are going to visit their children together.

Brenda is the first one to be greeted and she makes a beeline for Grandma Jenny. "Grandma, I was so sad to see you go, but I knew you wanted to be with grandpa, so I forgive you for leaving me."

"My dear sweet granddaughter you knew I would be leaving soon. Besides I couldn't leave your grandpa here to get our new home set up. He'd turn it into one big car garage." Cory stood there smiling and shaking his head up and down.

Tamla needed to talk with Margo. "Mom we are starting to have some serious problems on Earth."

"Like what?"

"Well, the governments are starting to break down on economic lines."

"What do you mean I thought there was a world economic system set up?"

"There is, I think the problem is that the few people who don't understand what's going on with Atlantis are starting to panic."

"Oh dear, I was afraid this would happen when the

Wayshowers were gone. You Indigos aren't really meant to deal with these problems."

"So what should we do?"

"The only thing you can do is to vibrate out as much love as you can and hope you can reach some of them."

Paul was right there and couldn't agree more. "Tamla you and Shasha have been an excellent team in politics before, now just turn that energy into helping your people to transition into the fourth dimension."

"Dad, how are we supposed to do that?"

"Teach them how to ascend to the fourth dimension, through love, and purity. Also you should enlist Brenda in this campaign, she knows all about the heart, and it's vibrations."

"Thanks dad, I'm sure you've taught Brenda well, and she will be an asset in helping through this time on Earth."

Margo woke up early in the morning, she noticed how beautiful the two moons were, and she wanted to write.

To Ascend

People on Earth let me tell you.
Prepare your Heart and Soul.
For life on Atlantis will be new.

Let go of your worldly things.
You see Atlantis in the sky.
Freedom for your Soul she brings.

To be young again is to be free.
Loving all who pass you by.
With friends who will always be.

Ascend to Atlantis to be.
Ascend to Atlantis you see.
Ascend to Atlantis and find.
Ascend to Heart from mind.

He had the most wonderful dream. He and his bride of well over 70 years were both young again. They were both in their mid to late 20's and very much in love. Waking up he rolled over to see Margo laying there facing the wall. These were his first words to her this morning "Dear, I had the most wonderful dream about us."

"You did huh, tell me about it."

Before he could answer she rolled over to face him and he proclaimed "it wasn't a dream, we are young again!" Paul was feeling more in love with her than he had in decades. "Margo we are spending the day together and it's going to be like it was in the late 60's for us." He then walked up to her, put his arm around her shoulder, leaned her back, and gave her a kiss to rival a soldier returning home from war.

With her heart beating and breathing in the love around her she said "dear you are the most romantic person on Atlantis. I love you so much."

Off to the mountains to go for a hike, flying around and looking for the perfect spot up high on a mountain. Margo spotted an area that appealed to her and said "Paul, there, there, right there, let's go down, and spend our afternoon there!" A quick right turn and then down for a landing.

"Perfect spot you found my dear." He then picked her up into his arms, spun her around, stopped, and looked her in the eyes and said. "My love you mean the world to me. Even the second one we are now on."

"Okay my handsome man let's find some lunch to eat."

Plenty of nuts, berries, and some rest it was then time to go for a hike. They were both so in tune with their home that all they could do was touch the trees, communicate with, and appreciate all that was around them. Paul's heart was bouncing and he said "hey let's ask this tree what its name is."

"Okay, first things first; tree can we touch you?"

The branches moved towards them in a hugging gesture, so Margo opened her arms, and hugged the tree. Paul joined in and said "what's your name?"

They both heard "Bill."

"Wow, Mr. Bill, I like it."

Then Bill said "that's Jennifer over there."

Now of course these names aren't in English, but in Atlantis everything is naturally translated for your understanding.

Done with hiking they decided to enjoy each other, and although love making is love making it is different in the fourth dimension, and it is in no way less enjoyable. It's probably even more exciting, sensual, and satisfyingly wonderful.

"Oh dear, you are so beautiful and I am so lucky to have met you at Woodstock in our other life."

She smiled and said "shut up and kiss me."

With this kiss Paul's emotions went into high gear. It felt like travelling through a black hole at light speed His thoughts were, *what a blessed and wonderful life, I am so happy I volunteered to go to Earth, and now I'm here in an even better place.*

After a swim in and out of the lakes, they went home, and made a promise to do this more often. Sitting out on their porch she was holding his hand with her heart feeling so happy. She sipped her tea and wrote.

My Love

There was a time when we knew.
Our days on Earth would be few.

Our lives would grow to find.
We need to practice to be kind.

Let your Heart lead and you may.
Understand your each and every day.

Not always easy to be believed.
I felt my Heart could be deceived.

It's funny to talk about the past now.
Unlike before we didn't know how.

Living this new life we can begin.
Because now that we are young again.

We now have a thousand years.
Move on from the past life of tears.

My Love is forever
My Lover is clever
My Lover would never
Cause our Love to Sever

See how they grow in Millennium Earth.

ABOUT THE AUTHOR

Kelly Fields was born in 1962 and moved to Florida from Texas at three. After high school he joined the Army as a Combat Engineer and a Paratrooper in the 82nd Airborne Div. He has been married for almost 30 years and has worked in the engineering field as a CAD engineer for over 30 years. He wrote this his first book in 2015 and currently is working on many more.

81774855R00127

Made in the USA
Lexington, KY
21 February 2018